The Dead Man's Message
An Occult Romance

by

Florence Marryat

edited with an introduction and notes by Greta
Depledge

Victorian Secrets 2009

Published by

Victorian Secrets Limited
32 Hanover Terrace
Brighton BN2 9SN

www.victoriansecrets.co.uk

The Dead Man's Message by Florence Marryat
First published in 1894
This Victorian Secrets edition 2009

Introduction and notes © 2009 by Greta Depledge
This edition © 2009 by Victorian Secrets

Composition and design by Catherine Pope
Cover photo © iStockphoto.com/appletat

A catalogue record for this book is available from the British
Library.

ISBN 978-1-906469-10-8

CONTENTS

Acknowledgements

I am grateful to Catherine Pope for her enterprise and ingenuity in setting up Victorian Secrets publishing house and thereby making the works of neglected and forgotten writers increasingly available to the modern reader. It is a wonderful enterprise and it is a pleasure to be involved.

I would like to dedicate this edition to the memory of Sally Ledger – a wonderful teacher, mentor and very dear friend. If, as Marryat believed, the spirits of our dear departed live on then, Sally, you will know how very much you are missed. Your wit, humour, intelligence and friendship were life enhancing. Thank you.

Greta Depledge, 2009

Introduction

1. The life and work of Florence Marryat

The life of Florence Marryat contains all the intrigue of one of her sensation fictions – marriage, adultery, separation, numerous children, bereavement, notoriety, fame and success. A glimpse of Marryat's life can, perhaps, be gained from her 1892 novel *The Nobler Sex* which is generally perceived as being her most auto-biographical work. It tells the story of a most eventful and dramatic life with a heroine who is admirable and infuriating in equal measure, but whose life is far from dull. The central protagonist of the novel is an unhappily (twice) married, successful author who converts to Catholicism and who finds comfort in spiritualism.

A book by Harry Furniss who was a regular contributor to the *London Society* journal during Marryat's reign as editor contains the following anecdote about Marryat's eventful life:

> Known as Mrs Ross Church when I first met her, she decided to marry someone else, and discarded her husband, who I think was in the army. Anyway, she sent all her friends and acquaintances, myself included, a statement in cold printers ink, informing us that she was not divorced, but that in future she wished to be known as Mrs Lean. This little piece of eccentricity fell into her husband's solicitor's hands and thus ended the Church business.[1]

Hardly surprising then that a woman so doggedly determined to follow her own path has left us with a collected works full of independent, strong-minded female characters.

That this prolific novelist, editor, journalist, actress and spiritualist is finally receiving critical interest is no surprise. What is perhaps surprising is that it has taken so long for academic attention to bring to light her long-neglected work. Florence Marryat was immensely popular with the reading public through-out her long and prolific career. Furniss in his book on Victorian

---

[1] Harry Furniss, *Some Victorian Women: Good, Bad and Indifferent* (London: John Lane, The Bodley Head Ltd, 1923), p. 11.

women writers describes her as "a prolific writer, but not a great one."[2] However, as her novels are now becoming increasingly available Marryat's work and this statement can be reassessed.

Whilst names like Mary Elizabeth Braddon, Marie Corelli, and Rhoda Broughton are now quite familiar, it is likely that many still have not heard of Marryat despite her prominent place in Victorian literary circles. Marryat's contribution to the 1892 collaborative novel *The Fate of Fenella* alongside such writers as Frances Eleanor Trollope, Arthur Conan Doyle, Bram Stoker, and many others gives us a clear indication of her literary standing at this time.[3] In fact, Marryat was familiar with literary circles from a young age. Her father's friendships with his leading literary contemporaries meant that Marryat was able to approach Charles Dickens for advice early in her career. The Marryat archive at Yale contains a letter from Dickens to Marryat with his detailed comments on her 1867 novel *The Confessions of Gerald Estcourt*. Her 1897 gothic tale *The Blood of the Vampire*, one of the few works by Marryat to have received some critical attention, was published the same year as Bram Stoker's *Dracula*. However, whilst *Dracula* has achieved the status of being probably the most regularly listed novel of all undergraduate courses in English Literary degree programmes, Marryat's novel of that same year is barely known – although I would suggest that the central female figure of this novel, Harriet Brandt, is as worthy of academic interest as her fictional vampiric sister, Lucy Westenra. All this builds a somewhat confusing frame of reference to our understanding of Marryat's prominence and then obscurity in the history of English literature.

It could perhaps be argued that Marryat initially established her career on the coat-tails of her successful father. Captain Marryat's sea-faring novels were hugely successful and Marryat's devotion to, and reverence of, her father is abundantly clear in her 1872 *Life and Letters of Captain Marryat*. Furthermore, despite having been married a number of years before her first novel was published Marryat

---

[2] Furniss, *Women*, p. 10.
[3] This collaborative work has recently been reprinted – see *The Fate of Fenella*, ed. by Andrew Maunder (Kansas City: Valancourt Books, 2008).

chose to publish in her maiden name. In an interview given in 1891 to Frederick Dolman for *Myra's Journal: The Lady's Monthly Magazine* when discussing her decision to try and get her first work *Love's Conflict* published by her father's publishers Bentley's she said "Mr Bentley, probably glad to have the name Marryat again on his books if they had any merit at all, sent me a cheque within a very short time."[4] Clearly it was an astute business decision to use her father's name and reputation to get her own career off the ground. Marryat's pride in her father's legacy and the influence he had on her is evident throughout her life and career. In this 1891 interview Dolman describes the memorabilia related to her father that Marryat kept in her study, he writes: "with these and many other things to keep alive the memory of her gallant father, it was not strange that at the close of our conversation the novelist should be speaking of him rather than of her own varied and interesting career."[5]

However Marryat's popularity and reputation were soon established and her literary talents came to be recognised in their own right. Her novels were regularly reviewed in many of the leading journals, and whilst some of the reviews appear somewhat double-edged her ability to write a readable story that readers would respond well to was regularly commented on. Marryat was, from the very beginning of her career, a very canny literary professional. She displayed an excellent astuteness for working her contemporary marketplace.

There is no obvious answer why a successful novelist like Marryat should have disappeared from the history of Victorian fiction in the way that she has. Andrew Maunder, in his excellent introduction to *Love's Conflict* for Pickering and Chatto's *Varieties of Women's Sensation Fiction* series, suggests that Marryat was aware of the 'ephemerality' of her own work and certainly that she has been, until now, largely out of print would support this assessment.[6]

---

[4] Frederick Dolman, 'Miss Florence Marryat at Home', *Myra's Journal: The Lady's Monthly Magazine* vol XVII, no. 5, (1891), pp. 1-2.

[5] Dolman, 'Marryat', *Myra's Journal: The Lady's Monthly Magazine* vol XVII, no. 5, (1891), pp. 1-2.

[6] Andrew Maunder (ed) *Love's Conflict*, in *Varieties of Women's Sensation Fiction 1855*

Marryat's novels of the 1860s such as *The Confessions of Gerald Estcourt, Love's Conflict, For Ever and Ever* and *Nelly Brooke* are typical of the sensation fiction that was so popular at that time and for which writers such as Mary Elizabeth Braddon became well-known. Marryat's books sold equally well, although Maunder's research has revealed that Marryat, in her early career, regularly felt that she was not paid as handsomely as many of her contemporaries.[7] So why Marryat is so far behind Braddon in terms of revival is curious. As Maunder rightly points out she was one of the most prolific writers of her time and her works were translated into a number of languages giving her international fame.[8] Clearly Marryat's style of writing would have become increasingly unfashionable as the modernist period developed in the early decades of the twentieth century. However, appreciation of her work is certainly due for a revival and is very relevant to the current academic trend for re-visiting forgotten and neglected Victorian popular novelists.

Whilst the novels which make up the greater part of Marryat's oeuvre do deal with classic sensation themes – adultery, bigamy, murder, seduction, madness – there is, throughout Marryat's writing, a strong vein of interesting and complex female characters. Unsurprisingly, given her own experiences of married life, raising and financially supporting her family, Marryat wrote about strong women but also about the vulnerability of women in the nineteenth-century marriage market.

Further to this, she does, in many of her novels, pay particular attention to the vulnerability of women at the hands of the medical profession and she engages with scientific and medical debates throughout her writing. This awareness of contemporary aspects of science and medicine warrants further academic study. *The Dead Man's Message* is one very good example of Marryat's engagement with the science of her day – more of which shortly.

Marryat's popularity, professional acumen in the literary market-

---

- *1890*, (London: Pickering and Chatto, 2004), vol 2, p. vii.
[7] Maunder, *Love's Conflict*, p. x.
[8] Maunder, *Love's Conflict*, p. vii.

place, the range of writing she produced, and her varied career should have guaranteed her an enduring place in the study of Victorian fiction. However, this was not to be the case. As Maunder wrote, quite rightly, in 2004: "The idea that anyone would ever want to write a book solely devoted to this eminent Victorian woman or even republish some of her work has seemed eccentric or at least unnecessary."[9] Thankfully 2009 sees a different picture emerging with Marryat's work appearing regularly on conference programmes, editions of a number of her novels becoming available and at least one book devoted to her life and work in the pipeline of an academic press.

Marryat's work most certainly warrants further academic interest and the publication of this curious little novella by Marryat is a welcome addition to the range of works, penned by this writer, which is currently available.

---

[9] Maunder, *Love's Conflict*, p. viii.

A Brief Chronology:

1833 (9th July) Born in Brighton. Parents were the former naval officer turned novelist Captain Frederick Marryat and Catherine (née Shairp).

1847 Brother, Frederick, drowned at sea.

1854 (13th June) Marryat married Thomas Ross Church, Ensign in the 12th Madras Staff Corps in Penang. She went on to have eight children by Ross Church, of whom seven survived in to adulthood.

1860 Marryat leaves Penang and returns to England pregnant with her fourth child. Ross Church travels regularly to see his family.

1861 Death of Florence Marryat's daughter, Florence, at the age of 10 days, (10th January).

1863 Begins writing *Love's Conflict* whilst nursing her children through scarlet fever.

1865 *Love's Conflict* is published by Bentley and Son. That year also saw the publication of *Too Good for Him* and *Woman Against Woman*.

1868 Publication of *Gup* – sketches of garrison life in India.

1872 Marryat publishes *The Life and Letters of Captain Marryat*.

1872 Begins her time as editor of *London Society*, a position she holds until 1876.

1872 First play *Miss Chester* produced.

1875 *Open! Sesame!* published.

1878 Sued for divorce by her husband Thomas Ross Church, who cited his wife's adultery with Colonel Francis Lean.

1879 Married Colonel Francis Lean – 5th June.

1881 *Her World Against a Lie* – Marryat became an actress performing in the above drama which she had written herself. The play was produced in London.

1882 Began touring with the D'Oyly Carte theatre company.

1886 *Tom Tiddler's Ground* published – an account of her travels in the United States of America.

1891 *There is No Death* published.

1892 Publication of *The Nobler Sex* regarded as Marryat's most auto-biographical novel.

1894 *The Spirit World* published.

1895 Marryat becomes very active in the recently formed Society of Authors.

1897 *The Blood of the Vampire* published.

1899 Died on the 27th October aged 66 due to complications from diabetes. Her funeral was held on 2nd November at the Church of Our Lady, St John's Wood. Marryat was buried at Kensal Green Cemetery.

2. *The Dead Man's Message* – a lesson in spirituality

Readers who do not wish to learn details of the plot might want to read the introduction afterwards.

Florence Marryat's spiritualist beliefs and practices have been well documented in her books *There is No Death* of 1891 and *The Spirit World* of 1894. Marryat claims, in *The Spirit World*, that her interest in the spiritual other was due to the influence of a family servant who introduced Florence to the idea that the spirits of the dead moved freely about the earth, when Florence was very young. The publication of *There is No Death* and *The Spirit World* caused a considerable stir and Marryat's openness about her spiritual beliefs and practices exposed her to considerable mockery. However, like many others committed to the phenomena of spiritualism, she remained committed to her beliefs until the end of her life and, presumably, beyond.

Her 1894 novella *The Dead Man's Message* is inspired by this fundamental belief in life after death and Marryat uses the text to propagate the message that sins in life will not go unpunished in the spirit world. The central protagonist, Professor Aldwyn, wakes, after what he believes was a nap, to discover that he is, in fact, dead. The Professor has entered the first sphere of the spirit world and experiences the humiliation of learning that his death has come as a blessed relief to his long suffering second wife and children.

The narrative trajectory of the novella is straightforward – the Professor is kept in one of the lowest levels of the spirit world and, accompanied by his spirit guide, is forced to acknowledge his earthly sins. Unsurprisingly the Professor learns repentance. The reader is told at the close of the novel that:

> on him there rested a bright ray of sunshine, a reflection of the smile which God had smiled upon his repentant child.

However, despite the brevity of this text, its engagement with contemporary debates makes it a rewarding study.

In the first instance, Marryat does highlight the vulnerable position of women at the mercy of tyrannical husbands. The

Professor's wife, Ethel, is the classic oppressed wife of an ostensibly stereotypical Victorian patriarchal male. Allowed no friends of her own, berated for her allegedly poor housekeeping skills, she is demeaned and belittled. But what is important about the Professor and what, I would suggest, is the central thread of this text is the Professor's status as a man of science.

This text juxtaposes the very oppositional forces of science and spiritualism and attempts to reconcile them. The interface of science, medicine and spiritualism in this novella reveals Marryat's awareness of, and engagement with, the extensive debates that were taking place in the second half of the nineteenth century – namely whether spiritualism could be accommodated in, or co-exist with, a continually evolving scientific understanding of the world. An editorial in the *Lancet* of 1860 states:

> What are the phenomena of Spiritualism? The most remarkable are table-rapping, table-moving, and clairvoyance. Odd people, having abundance of faith, – for we shall presently see that unquestioning credulity is the indispensable condition for appreciating these phenomena, – affirm (and we do not doubt them) that they hear tables rapped, and see them pirouette and dance, but do not see the rapper or the mysterious ballet-master. This is what they see and what they do not see. ... Formulized, the spiritual proposition is this: The table was seen to dance; tables do not dance unless some compelling power, physical or spiritual be applied to them; no physical power could be detected in action by the observer: therefore the moving power was spiritual. Q.E.D.

The editorial continues with a plethora of scientific logic, and concludes:

> We have adverted to this subject with a reluctance that amounts to loathing. It is a lamentable task to be called upon to notice seriously a moral epidemic, even upon a limited scale, which implies such an utter defect of reasoning power – such debasing superstition; and that, too, in men and women who claim to belong to the educated classes. In our self-conceit, we deplore the ignorance of our forefathers who hanged and drowned witches. But wherein lies the difference between the witches of old and the mediums of to-day? They do the same things, by

similar pretended agency, and what they do is of equal value to
society. We do not propose to hang mediums; but in the name of
common sense, and for the credit of the nineteenth century, let
them starve or find an honest livelihood.'[10]

In *The Dead Man's Message* Marryat challenges the scientific
establishment's cynical and dismissive attitude to spiritualism by
having a dedicated man of science undergo a spiritual awakening.
Professor Aldwyn is deeply immersed in scientific pursuits – he
neglects to be at his dying father's bedside because "he had been
employed on some very interesting and difficult scientific experiments." However, after his own death the Professor is forced to
believe in a world of spirits which his rational, scientific mind
would have previously dismissed. The message of this text is that
men of science should find a balance between these two worlds.
Marryat argues for their co-existence and mutual understanding.
Because of the growing popularity of spiritualism in the second
half of the nineteenth century the *Lancet* was forced to rethink its
dismissive attitude toward the subject. In 1876 we read:

> there are so many persons who, from different causes, in varying
> degrees and on diverse – almost contradictory – grounds declare
> themselves believers in spiritualism, that we think it expedient to
> treat the matter seriously, and, as far as may be possible, to give
> the subject that scientific consideration claimed for it.[11]

The *Lancet's* change of position on this matter is an indication of
just how widespread and popular spiritualism had become. The
British Association of Spiritualists was formed in 1873, many other
local societies developed and at least two spiritualist journals circu-
lated widely from the 1860s – *Human Nature* and the *Spiritualist*.[12]
Spiritualism rapidly became a widely discussed and controversial
subject, and one which the scientific community could not ignore.
    In the text we note with interest that the Professor's spirit guide

[10] *Lancet*, 20th October 1860, pp. 393-394.
[11] *Lancet*, 23rd September 1876, p. 431.
[12] See Alex Owen, *The Darkened Room: Women, Power and Spiritualism in Late
Victorian England* (Chicago & London: University of Chicago Press, 2004).

who, he is told, had been with him since he was born was:

> "A chemist and a scientist, like yourself. It is from my influence
> that your own proclivities arose. [but] Your eyes have been too
> much fixed on yourself and your pursuits, to feel a spiritual
> influence. The spirituality in you has been neglected…"

The spirit guide has found a balance between the seemingly oppositional forces and offers the Professor one last chance to, quite
literally, save his soul.

This little known novella of Marryat's does, of course, prefigure
a more well-known fictional text which depicts a sceptical man of
science being forced to acknowledge the power and presence of
the spiritual other. One of the most well-known scientific and
literary brains to embrace spiritualism was Arthur Conan Doyle – a
qualified, and at one stage, practising physician. His work, *The Land
of Mist,* contains that most famous man of science, Professor
Challenger, becoming involved in spiritualist investigations and,
reluctantly, becoming a believer. In his own life, Doyle epitomised
the co-existence of science and spiritualism that Marryat is clearly
advocating in this text. Like many others Doyle, and Marryat,
argued for the science *of* spiritualism. Indeed, Doyle used his
medical knowledge to validate spiritualist activities. He believed
that recording the pulse of a medium throughout a sitting would
provide an excellent check against fraud, and reported on one particular medium whose pulse went up to a very satisfactory 127
during a trance from a normal of 78.[13] This experiment was written
up in 1923, 27 years after the publication of *The Dead Man's Message.*
Clearly the debate between science and spiritualism that Marryat
plays out in her novella remained topical over a significant period
of time, seemingly never resolved to the satisfaction of either side.

Many eminent scientific figures became involved in trying to
prove that spiritualism was a creditable science. One such notable
person was the celebrated naturalist Alfred Russel Wallace, whose
belief in spiritualism supported him through his grief when his six

---

[13] Robin A E & Key J D, *Medical Casebook of Doctor Arthur Conan Doyle* (Florida: R
E Krieger Inc, 1984), p.70.

year old son died. However, despite his reputation within the scientific community his writings in support of spiritualism were lamented by his peers, as seen in an editorial in the *Lancet* in 1874:

> We commend to our readers in search of the marvellous two papers written by Mr Alfred Wallace in the May and June numbers of the Fortnightly Review 'On Modern Spiritualism'. In these the most astounding statements are made with such calm assurance and confidence that we are really at at a loss to say whether the general experience of the human race is to be cast aside as worthless, or whether we are to admit the possibility of events taking place which are in point of fact miracles, and which are stated to be vouched for by large numbers of men who, apparently possessing sound faculties, have commenced as sceptics, have used every effort to discover deception, and have ended by becoming believers.'[14]

The tone of the *Lancet* was representative of so many in the scientific community who believed that the world of the spirit and the world of documented scientific proof and reasoning were ideologically incompatible. In 1894 the *Lancet* is still struggling with Wallace's ongoing and public support of spiritualism:

> That Dr Alfred Russel Wallace is a very distinguished savant no one who knows aught of science will deny. ... In many respects Dr. Wallace is a really great man and we are profoundly sorry that his greatness should have mingled with it such weaknesses as are exhibited in his dealings with subjects like anti-vaccination and demonology. ... But Dr. Wallace's reputation is so great and so thoroughly well deserved that it will long outlast the memory of his weaknesses, much as these are now apt to be in evidence. He will go down to posterity as a most distinguished savant whose name will have to be classed [with] those of Darwin and Spencer, while his eccentricities ... will be buried in a kindly oblivion.'[15]

Wallace's 1896 book *Miracles and Modern Spiritualism* is a lengthy tract in which he validates various spiritual phenomena by giving examples of his own spiritualist experiences and discussing and

---

[14] *Lancet*, 13th June 1874, p. 843
[15] *Lancet*, 14th July 1894, p. 88.

quoting other men of science who are also believers. He writes:

> Now what do our leaders of public opinion say when a scientific
> man of proved ability again observes a large portion of the more
> extraordinary phenomena, in his own house, under test
> conditions, and affirms their objective reality; and this not after a
> hasty examination, but after four years of research? Men "with
> heavy scientific appendages to their names" refuse to examine
> them when invited; the eminent society of which he is a fellow
> refuses to record them; and the press cries out that it wants better
> witnesses ... and that such facts want 'confirmation' before they
> can be believed. But why more confirmation? And when again
> 'confirmed', who is to confirm the confirmer.[16]

For Marryat's fictional character the confirmation of the phenomena comes in experiencing it first-hand. Aldwyn is a man of
science who undergoes a spiritual awakening and he is forced to
acknowledge that his dispassionate scientific reasoning must also
allow for the spiritual other. His final acceptance of a spirit life
engages with the debate that was being played out in scientific
circles. Aldwyn experiences the spiritual awakening that Wallace
wishes to convince the scathing scientific community the validity
of. In Wallace science and spirituality did co-exist and Marryat
looks to harmonise the real with the supposedly surreal in this
fascinating little text.

Marryat gives her readers an insight in to the many dimensions
of the spirit world in this novella. The sphere in which Professor
Aldwyn is first confined on entering the spirit world is one of the
lowest. He is tormented with glimpses of the higher spheres when
his spirit guide shows him his first wife and the children of that
marriage who miscarried or were stillborn, now grown and healthy,
playing with their mother. That children could grow and age in the
spirit world is something that Marryat allegedly discovered after
her own experience – detailed in *There is No Death* – of seeing her
spirit child Florence appear to her, grown and healthy despite

---

[16] Alfred R Wallace, *Miracles and Modern Spiritualism* (London: George Redway,
1896), p. 210.

having left the earthly world as a 10 day old baby.[17] In *The Dead Man's Message* Marryat utilises what she had previously narrated as a very personal experience in order to make the Professor's spiritual journey more poignant. The professor cannot join his wife and children until he atones for his sins.

Aldwyn is, however, not alone in his lowly sphere. He is, in fact, surrounded by animals in this sphere of the spirit world. And this, admittedly brief moment in the text, opens up another avenue of contemporary scientific debate with which Marryat engages. Aldwyn asks his spirit guide: "what are these animals that cling so persistently about my feet?" He is told:

> "These are the spirits of the dumb brutes whom you tortured in the name of science. These are the dogs, and rabbits, and cats which you vivisected for your own curiosity, and who died agonizing, lingering deaths under your cruel hands." ...

> "God, who made these creatures for our pleasure and our use, never intended them to minister to our discoveries, in science or anything else, by means of horrors too terrible to think of. All the long, weary hours of acute pain under which you kept these helpless creatures of God, in order that you might watch their hearts beating, or the various parts of their organism working, have been reckoned up against you, and the animals themselves are ordained to accompany you throughout the hell you have created for yourself, till your own tortures will have so accumulated that you would be thankful to exchange them for those you made them suffer—aye, even to have your head and body laid out and secured on the vivisecting table, as theirs were, whilst all your nerves and most of the delicate portions of your system are mutilated by the dissecting knife. ...No it is useless for you to try to kick them away. You can no longer harm them and they are under God's orders, and not yours. Be thankful if you are not condemned to go through what you made them suffer."

This is, without doubt, very emotive writing. The vivisection debate in the late nineteenth century was extensive and passionate. Through this brief allusion to the Professor's vivisection practices Marryat contextualises many of the concerns that surrounded the

---

[17] See Appendix C.

experimental scientist. Other fictional representations of the vivi-sector in nineteenth century literature have highlighted the brutality of which he was allegedly capable – Dr Benjulia in Wilkie Collins's *Heart and Science* (1883) and Dan McClure, the husband of the eponymous heroine in Sarah Grand's *The Beth Book* (1897). The perceived brutality of the vivisector was writ large in writing of the time. A near-contemporary anti-vivisection pamphlet states:

> In the interests of medicine, because participation in such practices must harden and coarsen all in any way engaged in or consenting to them, must dehumanize both actors and spectators and disqualify them for the sympathetic discharge of the duties of their beneficent profession.[18]

Sarah Grand's Beth leaves her husband when she discovers he practices vivisection:

> "Had I known you were a vivisector, I should not only have refused to marry you, I should have declined to associate with you. To conceal such a thing from the woman you were about to marry was a cruel injustice – a fraud!"[19]

Similarly, in John Davidson's 1901 poem 'The Testament of a Vivisector' the vivisector confesses 'I live alone – my wife Forsook me'.[20]

Aldwyn's bullying treatment of his wife, referred to earlier is, then, more than a stereotypical portrayal of the domineering Victorian patriarch but is rather a configuration of the brutality the vivisector was allegedly capable of. Ethel learns from one of the Professor's colleagues that her husband:

> boasted to his male acquaintances how he had curbed and broken your spirit, as he did that of the dumb brutes in his vivisecting

---

[18] Anthony George Shiell, *Dogs and Their Dissectors: Addresses on Vivisection* (Brighton: W.J. Smith, 1903), p 7.
[19] Sarah Grand, *The Beth Book* (1893, repr. London: Virago Press, 1980), p. 441.
[20] John Davidson, *Testaments. No. 1 The Testament of a Vivisector* (London: Grant Richards, 1901).

> trough, until you knew no will but his own; who was so mean, that he would not spend as much on your pleasure in a year as he did on his own experiments in a day.

The antivivisection stance is clear – and links between spiritualists and antivivisectionists throughout the nineteenth century are well documented: all living creatures were sacred and deserved to be treated with dignity. The successful professional spiritualist Chandos Leigh Hunt was an active anti-vivisectionist and, like Wallace, was also very involved in the anti-vaccination campaigns.[21] Conan Doyle, late in life, wrote about the vivisection that was an inevitable part of his medical training – reflecting particularly on one of his professors:

> He was, I fear, a rather ruthless vivisector, and though I have always recognized that a minimum of painless vivisection is necessary, and far more justifiable than the eating of meat as a food, I am glad that the law was made more stringent so as to restrain such men as he.[22]

Conan Doyle is clearly attempting to reconcile his spiritual beliefs with scientific necessity, advocating the minimum of vivisection that it was believed was necessary for scientific advance. Marryat is less able to tolerate the idea of vivisection at any level but throughout this story does try to reconcile aspects of contemporary science with the spiritual other. Rather than debunking or dismissing science's skepticism of spiritualism it would seem that she does want the validity that scientific acknowledgement could bring. In *There is No Death* she writes somewhat tentatively that some men of science have recognized spiritualism and in this novella the Professor, by the end of the story, reflects those enlightened scientific minds.

However, Marryat does not confine spiritual awakening in this novel to just the Professor. His wife and daughter also have the 'other world' opened up to them. Aldwyn's daughter, Maddy, has a

21 Owen, *Darkened Room*, pp. 123-137.
22 *Medical Casebook,* p.70.

photograph taken and the developed picture shows the form of a woman standing with her. Ethel recognizes the woman to be the Professor's first wife – Maddy's mother. Her spiritual presence in Maddy's life is confirmed when they visit a medium. Given Marryat's telling in *The Spirit World* of how a servant introduced her to ideas of the spiritual other it is interesting to note in this novella that the medium whom Ethel and Maddy visit is, in fact, a former servant of Ethel's parents who:

> was always rather a strange girl – uncanny, mother used to call her. She could tell the cards in the most wonderful manner, and everything she foretold through them came true, until the villagers used to ask her to lay them on every occasion, and mother was obliged to forbid her doing so, it became such a nuisance. She had wonderful eyes too, quite different from those of other people, and was able to foretell if invalids would live or die, and whether the harvest would fail or be fruitful, and all sorts of curious things. I was very young when she lived with us, and they kept the knowledge from me, but I heard the stories afterwards from others.[23]

Spirit photography was, of course, just one of the many very contentious spiritual phenomena that fed the debate surrounding the truth of spiritualism throughout the years. Scientists who supported the phenomenon engaged in extensive debate with those who denounced it. William Mumler is credited with having taken the first spirit photograph in America in 1861. Most famously he claims to have taken one of President Lincoln standing with his hand protectively on the shoulder of his widow.[24] Marryat documents her own experiences of spirit photography in *There is No Death.*[25] In this novella the validity of the spirit photography is accepted with very little questioning.

Alfred Wallace wrote extensively in support of spirit photo-

---

[23] For a further discussion of how spiritualism and mediumship offered opportunities for social mobility to the lower classers see Owen, *The Darkened Room.*
[24] See Major Tom Patterson, *100 Years of Spirit Photography* (London: Regency Press, 1965).
[25] See Appendix C.

raphy. His belief in the integrity of the famous spirit photographers was given as concluding fact of the objective existence of invisible human forms:

> Through an independent set of most competent observers we have the crucial test of photography; a witness which cannot be deceived, which has no preconceived opinions, which cannot register 'subjective' impressions; a thoroughly scientific witness.[26]

The *Lancet,* unsurprisingly, was less believing:

> – dim spectral forms, shadowy semblances of the dead, that look not like the inhabitants o' th' earth and yet are on't, have positively consented, at the bidding of a poor mortal, to sit in the photographer's chair and allowed their cartes de visite to be taken. It has been reserved for English experimenters to penetrate that region where "entity and quiddity the ghosts of defunct bodies fly" to pose, focus, and obtain a negative of a real, genuine, unmistakable spectre, with marrowless bones and (if any) cold blood.[27]

The *British Journal of Photography* gave extensive column inches to the phenomena throughout 1872 and 1873 – they were largely dismissive of the idea but many letters from those who believed in the phenomena were printed. The level of skepticism that was evident in many of the leading journals of the day such as the *British Journal of Photography* and, more significantly, the *Lancet* is hardly surprising. These supposed bastions of established scientific truth and fact seem as confirmed in their opposition as supports of spiritualism were in their belief. Reading through the – and I use the term loosely – 'evidence' from both sides one sees that there are levels of entrenchment and conviction that neither side seems capable of moving from. The *Lancet's* belief that most spiritualists, mediums and believers would be more correctly diagnosed as hysterics is well established. The acceptance of spiritualism by Aldwyn's wife and daughter, the female medium they visit, could

---

[26] Wallace, *Miracles*, p. 211.
[27] Lancet, 13th June 1874, p. 843.

all be dismissed as examples of the hysterical women the *Lancet* was ever ready to diagnose. Marryat, however, delivers her most pointed challenge to scientific skepticism through the conversion of one of their own – a confirmed skeptic, a scientist and perhaps most importantly, a man.

This short novella is, perhaps, first and foremost, a warning to those who neglect their spiritual needs. Marryat's own conviction in the validity of spiritualism does mean that the configuration of the professor's conversion is perhaps less than subtle. The spiritualist dogma is a little heavy-handed but the depiction of the earthly living characters – such as Ethel and Maddy are well done and representative of other women in Marryat's wider writing. By the time this novella appeared *There is No Death* had been in circulation for three years and Marryat was, the same year as *The Dead Man's Message,* to publish *The Spirit World.* So, in amongst much longer works on spiritualism and her other fictional works Marryat presents us with a novella in which she engages with humane questions over how people live their lives and contextualizes this within a story which grapples with much wider scientific debates. This text could, on the surface, be considered a curious little gothic tale but is, I would argue, a sometimes playful but engaging challenge to the wider scientific community and their skepticism of the spiritual other.

Suggestions for further reading

Harry Furniss, *Some Victorian Women: Good, Bad and Indifferent* (London: John Lane, The Bodley Head Ltd, 1923)

Florence Marryat, *There is No Death* (New York: Cosimo Classics, 2004).

Florence Marryat, *The Spirit World*, (London: White & Co, 1894).

Andrew Maunder (ed) *Love's Conflict*, in *Varieties of Women's Sensation Fiction 1855 – 1890*, (London: Pickering and Chatto, 2004), vol 2.

William H Mumler, *The Personal Experiences of William. H. Mumler in Spirit-Photography. Written by Himself* (Boston: Colby & Rich, 1875).

Janet Oppenheim, *The Other World: spiritualism and psychical research in England 1850 – 1914* (Cambridge: Cambridge University Press, 1985).

Alex Owen, *The Darkened Room: Women, Power and Spiritualism in Late Victorian England* (Chicago: University of Chicago Press, 2004).

Major Tom Patterson, *100 Years of Spirit Photography* (London: Regency Press, 1965).

Frank Podmore, *Modern Spiritualism: A History and a Criticism* vol ii (London: Methuen & Co, 1902).

Alfred R Wallace, *Miracles and Modern Spiritualism* (London: George Redway, 1896).

A Note on the text

This novella was first published in one volume in New York in 1894 by C. B. Reed. It was subsequently published in London in 1898 by Bliss Sands & Co., under the title of *A Soul on Fire.**

---

* Many thanks are due to Richard Beaton for his invaluable assistance on the publication history.

The Dead Man's Message

"Is Heaven a place or state of mind?
Let old experience tell.
Love carries Heaven where'er it goes,
And Hatred carries Hell."—CHARLES MACKAY.*

---

* From 'Heaven and Hell' by Charles Mackay.   Published in *Interludes and Undertones; or Music at Twilight*, (London: Chatto & Windus, 1884).

- CHAPTER ONE -

THE PROFESSOR IN THE BOSOM OF HIS FAMILY

Professor Aldwyn was seated in his library, deeply absorbed in the perusal of an article in the latest number of the *Fin du Siècle* magazine, his slippered feet stretched out on a velvet footstool before him, in front of a blazing fire. It was a magnificent fire. The crisp, frosty March air made the huge logs crackle and burn till the fiery sparks flew up the wide chimney in a shower of brilliance. The Professor's easy chair was the very easiest that can be imagined: under his head was a little crimson plush bolster that fitted into the hollow of his neck, and his ample dressing-gown folded over his figure in the most luxurious fashion. In fact, the Professor may be said to have been completely comfortable.

The room which he occupied evinced signs of wealth and good taste. It was almost lined with books; from the ceiling to the floor were rows and rows of shelves filled with valuable and well-bound volumes, collected by their owner during the entire period of his life, which had now extended over some five and fifty years. The Professor lived in his books; he cared for nothing else. He may almost be said to have eaten and drank books, for he seldom appeared at the domestic meals without one in his hands, which he would prop up against a tumbler or a cruet stand in front of him, and devour, in turn, with his dinner.

The carpet of the library was of rich, velvet pile; the writing table, capacious and fitted with every necessary and convenience; the chairs and sofas were substantial and luxurious. Heavy curtains shaded the windows and door, and two large argand lamps[1] lighted the room by night. But, further than this, there was no elegance

---

[1] Argand lamps invented in 1780 were a big improvement on previous oil lamps but were eventually superseded by the invention of kerosene lamps in the 1850s.

about the Professor's library; no flowers, nor dainty little tables, nor signs of feminine occupation were scattered about. It was essentially a man's room—but the room of a man who knew how to look after himself. Professor Aldwyn lay back in his chair, with his pale-blue eyes, assisted by spectacles, gazing intently at his book. The article that riveted his attention was entitled, "Is Self-delusion Insanity?" And, as he devoured it, he kept on making low murmurs of appreciation and acquiescence.

"Very good! True, quite true. I must talk the matter over with Bunster; and I should like to hear what Robson has to say on the subject. I will send them a wire to come in this evening, and we'll argue it out together."

And the Professor stretched out his feet still nearer to the generous, grateful fire, and revelled in its warmth. At this moment, there sounded a tap on the library door, a timid, hesitating tap, as if the tapper were not at all certain of the reception that would follow it.

"Come in!" growled the Professor.

The door opened, and on the threshold stood one of the prettiest young women to be seen in a day's march. She was tall and slender, with a fair complexion tinted like a wild rose, and soft, brown eyes, full of soul, and the capability of loving. This was Mrs. Aldwyn, the Professor's second wife, to whom he had been married for only two years.

"What is it?" he asked, petulantly. "Don't stand there with the door open! You are letting the most horrible draught into the room. Do, for goodness' sake, either come in, or go away again!"

The girl—she was not much more, only four and twenty—entered the room at once, and shut the door behind her, and then advanced a little towards his chair.

"I am sorry to disturb you, Henry," she began, "and I will not detain you a moment; only I have just received this wire"[2]—holding out a yellow envelope to him—"from my cousin Ned. He

---

[2] The inventors of the electric telegraph system were William Cooke and Charles Wheatstone. The system was first demonstrated in 1837 in London. By the end of the nineteenth century towns and villages across the country were connected by telegraph wires.

has returned from sea, you know, and he wants to come and see me this evening. What shall I say in answer? May I ask him to dinner?"

The Professor veered round in his chair and looked at her. He was a long, thin man, of rather a spare and ascetic appearance, notwithstanding his love of creature comforts; and his pale-blue eyes peered at Mrs. Aldwyn through his glasses, as if he had detected or wished to detect her in a crime.

"Why?" he demanded, curtly.

His wife commenced to stammer. "O! for no particular reason; only he is my first cousin, you know. We have not met for more than a year, and he wants to come. That's all!"

"Then he had better wait till he's asked. We can't have him to-night. It is not convenient! Mr. Bunster and Mr. Robson are coming to dine with us."

"Have you asked them? You never told me."

"No; but I am going to ask them now. Stay a minute, and you can take the notes and send them by James."

He turned to his writing-table, as he spoke, and commenced to write the notes of invitation. Having finished them, he handed them to his wife, and, without further comment, redirected his attention to his magazine article. Mrs. Aldwyn stood at the door a moment, twisting about the letters in her hand.

"But, Henry," she ventured to say, at last, "if we are to entertain these two gentlemen, it will not make much difference if I ask Ned Standish as well."

"Not make much difference! What are you talking about? Do you suppose, when I invite my scientific friends here to discuss some important question, that I want a jibbering donkey like Ned Standish to interrupt us with his nonsense? I won't have him. You must send a wire and say you are engaged, and that he must call some other time. Though what you want to see him at all for, I can't imagine."

"I don't often see any of my relations," replied his wife, with a quivering lip, "nor do I often trouble you with a request on the subject. Ned will not be in town over a few days, and he says he may not have another opportunity of calling."

4

"Well, he can't come to-night, and that's enough of it. It would destroy all my talk with my own friends. And I cannot understand, either, why you should always be hankering after your family in this childish manner. You have Madeline and Gilbert for companions. Why cannot you find your pleasure in them?"

Ethel Aldwyn made no further remonstrance, but left the room, closing the door rather sharply behind her. As she reached the hall, a handsome girl of about eighteen opened the dining-room door and confronted her.

"What did he say, Mumsey?" she asked. "Beastly, as usual?"

Mrs. Aldwyn gave a sad smile.

"I suppose you would say so, Maddy."

"He won't let me ask Ned to dinner, because he is going to have Mr. Bunster and Mr. Robson to spend the evening with himself."

"And what harm could nice, dear cousin Ned have done to those two horrid, old fogies? He would have been the only bright spot in the entertainment. But isn't it just like papa? He always opposes us in every possible way. Upon my word, I am beginning almost to hate him."

"Hush, hush, Maddy; you mustn't say that. It is wicked."

"Yes, Mumsey; I know that's always your cry; but how can you expect me to love or respect a man who lives only to cross us? What enjoyment do you ever have of your life, poor, dear thing? You know you're just as miserable as you can be."

"O, no; I'm not," replied Mrs. Aldwyn, winking away the suspicion of a tear. "Papa has every right to have things as he chooses. He is the master of the house; you must not forget that."

"And a nice master, too!" exclaimed Madeline, "living only to make everybody wretched. As for Gilbert, Mumsey, I believe he will murder his father some day, if he doesn't take care. He's perfectly bloodthirsty. You should have heard him talk last night. He says, if it goes on much longer, he shall run away from home."

"O! that's very naughty of Gilbert," exclaimed Mrs. Aldwyn, in a concerned voice; "I must talk to him about it. There will be a terrible quarrel some day if your father hears of any of his speeches. But take these notes and this telegram to James, Maddy dear, and tell him to deliver them at once. There's sixpence for the wire."

"And, I suppose, it's to tell that dear, handsome cousin Ned that he's not to come to-night," said Madeline, in a disappointed tone.

"Of course, my dear child," replied her step-mother, gravely; "what else should I say after your father's decision?"

Maddy made a grimace and ran off, and Mrs. Aldwyn passed into the dining-room, where Gilbert, a lad of sixteen, sat, in a discontented mood, before the fire. She felt very miserable as she did so. She dared not openly display her sympathy with the son and daughter of the house, but she felt their position and her own keenly. They were far bolder than herself, and criticised their father's selfishness and utter disregard of their feelings openly; but she dared not imitate them, though she knew they were right in their judgment of the Professor's character. For the sake of domestic peace, and in order to show Madeline and Gilbert a good example, she tried hard to hide what she thought of her husband's conduct in her own breast; but she often felt that life was too hard for her. To be placed, at her age, as the sole influence for good, over two grown-up and discontented children, when she so sorely needed a mother's guidance and counsel herself, was a very trying position for a young woman of four and twenty. But Gilbert and Madeline were very fond of her, and that was her great reward.

"O, Gilbert!" she exclaimed, as she saw the lad seize the coal scoop and throw a good load of fuel on the fire, "be careful; there's a dear boy. If papa saw you heaping up the coals in that fashion he would read us a lecture on economy. And coals have been fearfully dear this year, you know."

"He doesn't spare them on his own fire," replied the boy, as he threw on another shovelful, "so why are we to perish of cold? James told me he took in three scuttles of coals to the library yesterday. Professor Aldwyn likes to keep his toes warm; so does Professor Aldwyn's son. Bad luck to it! I wish I was the son of anybody else!"

"Don't say that, dear," replied Ethel, soothingly. "If you were not his son you would not be your mother's, and, I am sure, you would never wish that."

"It's a good thing she's dead," said the lad, doggedly, "and my only wonder is how he ever persuaded you, poor little Mumsey, to take her place. If she had been alive, she would have warned you not."

"Gilbert, it does make me so unhappy to hear you talk like that," replied Mrs. Aldwyn and, at that moment, the Professor entered the room.

"Why are you not at college?" he demanded of his son; but Gilbert made no answer.

"Gilbert, dear, your father speaks to you," interposed Ethel, with a look of alarm. She had come to be so frightened, poor girl, of the constant squabbling that took place between her husband and his children.

"I heard him," said the lad, insolently.

"Then why don't you answer me, sir?" exclaimed the Professor, angrily. "Why are you not at school?"

"Because you told me, last night, that I was such an ass, and an idiot, and a fool, that you were sick of paying the college fees for me, and that I had better take a broom and sweep a crossing, for I was fit for nothing else," responded his son.

"Then why haven't you taken the hint, and done as I advised you?" said the father.

"Henry! Henry!" said his wife, in a tone of expostulation.

"Don't you attempt to interfere, Ethel, between my children and myself, for you will do neither them nor yourself any good by it," exclaimed the Professor. "This lad is incorrigibly lazy and insolent, and he must be kept in check. Look at him now, as he sits there, with his rough hair and his dirty hands! Do you suppose I am going to sit down to luncheon with a savage like that? Go to your room, sir, and make yourself decent. And what do you mean by heaping coals on the fire? Isn't it enough that I have all the expense of your sister and yourself on my hands, that you must add to it by wasting my substance in that fashion? Take them off at once!"

"Take them off yourself!" cried the boy, as he darted from his seat and left the room.

"Is this some of your doing?" inquired the Professor of his wife.

"I think you might do me more justice than that, Henry," she replied. "Maddy and Gilbert would both tell you that I never encouraged either of them in rebellion against you."

She sat down at the table as she spoke. Her heart was bursting with a sense of unkindness and injustice, and her sympathy was all with the poor boy, who had known no better way of expressing his disapproval of the domestic tyranny that went on in the house, morning, noon and night, and made the children of this man hate and despise him.

Madeline now ran into the room, fresh from having encountered her brother on the stair. She was much the more determined spirit of the two, as she possessed the more vigorous frame and constitution. She threw one glance of defiance at her father, and then walked straight up to her step-mother and kissed her.

"What's the matter, Mumsey?" she asked. "No fresh worry, is there?"

"I consider that a most impertinent way of speaking," said the Professor, frowning. "What do you mean, Miss, by no 'fresh worry'?"

"Just what I said, papa. Mumsey looks sad; so I asked if it were due to a stale worry, or a fresh one. It's plain enough English, isn't it?"

"I cannot understand why you should ask your mamma such a question at all," was the irritable reply. "What worries have you to complain of, Ethel, fresh or stale?"

"Don't you think we have had sufficient argument?" said Mrs. Aldwyn, as she looked up and tried to smile. "Let us take our luncheon now. It is past the usual time. What will you have, Henry? Cutlets or mince?"

"Mince! cutlets!" repeated the Professor, with a sneer; "both warmed up from yesterday. How many times have I told you that I don't care how plain my meals are; no man ever cared less for eating than I do; but I cannot stand *réchauffés*.[3] They are perfectly tasteless to me. I would rather have dry bread."

"Here it is, papa," said Maddy, passing him the loaf.

---

[3] Warmed leftovers

"They are not so nice as fresh-cooked *plats*,[4] perhaps," said Mrs. Aldwyn; "though, I think, cook is very careful about warming them again; but they are far less expensive, you know, Henry, and you often complain of my housekeeping bills, as it is."

"Well, let the children eat them, then, and give me something fresh, a sweetbread[5] or a curry; it matters little, so that I can eat it; but I cannot digest those over-cooked dishes. They disagree with me."

"So they do with me," exclaimed Maddy, pushing her plate away. "If you can't eat them, no more can I. I must have inherited your fastidious liver; so you had better fork out some more house-keeping money for Mumsey, forthwith."

"Is this intended for impertinence?" demanded the Professor, grandly.

"O! dear me, no!" exclaimed his daughter. "It's only an example of heredity."

"What have you for dinner this evening?" he said, professing not to hear Maddy's answer, and turning to his Wife.

"Turbot, roast lamb, and macaroni," she answered.

"You are not going to ask my friends, Bunster and Robson, to sit down to a dinner like that, I hope. They are coming to have an important discussion with me on a scientific subject. We must feed them well."

"What additions do you wish me to make?"

"Soup, for one, then game to follow the lamb, sweets, and dessert. And have a bottle or two of champagne from the cellar— right-hand bin, number 18. And I don't want the children to dine at table to-night. Let them make their dinner now."

"But why didn't you say so before, Henry," she expostulated. "Gilbert has had no dinner at all, and Maddy next to nothing."

"Let her sit down and make it now, then," said the Professor; "and, as for that young brute upstairs, let him go without till he learns to treat me with proper respect. I'll ship him off to sea in

---

[4] These were a new dish that was created out of leftovers rather than simply reheating and reserving what was left of the original dish.

[5] Traditionally made from either the thymus gland or the pancreas of animals such as calf or lamb.

the next collier[6] I hear of, if he doesn't take care."

"And why am I not to dine down-stairs to-night?" asked Madeline.

"Because I don't choose that you shall," was the only reply she got, as her father left the room.

As the door closed, Maddy made a mock respectful curtsy to him, with her fingers to her nose.

"O! you *dear!*" she exclaimed; "you nice, loving, careful father! You ought to have a statue erected to you, you ought. Why, you haven't as much feeling for your children as a cat has for her kittens. Ugh if I thought I could ever behave like that to mine, I would go and hang myself before I had any."

She snapped her fingers twice or thrice at the closed door, and then, turning to see how her step-mother was taking her rebellious conduct, she perceived that she had laid her head down on her outstretched arms, and was quietly crying to herself.

"O! Mumsey, Mumsey!" cried Maddy, flying to her side, "what a beast I am to have made you cry! But I cannot love him, dear; it is no use. I cannot! I cannot!"

"It seems all so hopeless," sighed Mrs. Aldwyn, "and I feel so for poor Gilbert. What is to be done for the boy? Where will it all end?"

"Let's run away, the whole lot of us together," suggested Maddy; "I'll come, for one, and we should be happier working for our bread than obliged to bear his tempers, day after day. Do think of it, Mumsey."

"No, dearest, we mustn't even think of it. It's wicked. We haven't placed ourselves in this position—at least you and Gilbert haven't—and so you must do your duty till God pleases to show you a way out of it. It won't be for long, Maddy, you know. You are sure to marry some day, and Gilbert will go out into the world; and, then, you will both be free to make your own lives."

"And leave you here, poor darling, to bear it all by yourself," exclaimed the warm-hearted girl. "That would be a shame. Why, it would be enough to kill anybody."

---

[6] A bulk cargo ship.

For an answer, Ethel put her face down on the table, and began to sob.

"It was my own fault, my own fault," she murmured, "and I must bear it as best I can. O, Maddy, be careful how you marry. Keep a good man's love when you get it. Keep it as the greatest treasure of your life."

They were crying, quietly, in each others' arms, when a fearful tumult in the hall made them start to their feet.

"How dare you?" they heard Gilbert's voice exclaim; "What have I done that you should strike me? I have borne it from no man yet, and I will not bear it from you."

Ethel and Maddy ran to the door, and opened it at once. There stood Gilbert, his eyes flashing with rage, and his coat thrown off, as if he intended to close in with the Professor, and give him a thrashing.

"Gilbert, Gilbert, what are you doing?" cried Ethel, as she flew towards him. "Think where you are, and who you are speaking to."

"Leave me alone," replied the lad, shaking off her detaining arm; "I will brook no interference in this matter. My father has treated me like a brute, and he must give me an account of it. He found me in the kitchen having some luncheon, and he accused me of stealing and wasting his property; and, when I answered him, he struck me with that cane, and I won't bear it; I won't."

"O, Henry, it is not possible," exclaimed his wife, in distress.

"It is quite possible. If luncheon is laid for him in the dining-room, which he refuses to eat, and then he steals from the larder what may be intended for another meal, he *is* wasting my property, and I shall chastise him for it as I think fit," replied the Professor, still brandishing the cane in his hand.

"No, you won't," cried the lad defiantly; "you've thrashed me for the last time. If you attempt to touch me again, I'll give you a jolly good licking, father or no father."

"Are you sure I *am* your father?" demanded the Professor, in a sneering tone. "I should not like to swear to it myself. You may be the son of my next door neighbour, for aught I know. You have never shown signs of having any blood of mine in your veins."

This insult to his dead mother seemed to make all the blood in the boy's body boil, and swell his figure to twice its size. He advanced close to his father's side, and hissed in his ear—"You coward. You double-dyed coward and liar, to try and vilify my mother's name. Take that," and he struck the Professor straight across the mouth.

Ethel and Maddy screamed. They thought there would be bloodshed between the father and son; but the Professor, instead of wielding the stick again, turned very pale and trembled.

"You pitiful coward!" repeated Gilbert, "I would beg my bread from door to door before I would eat another crust at the expense of the defamer of my dead mother. Do you remember the text, 'And in hell he lifted up his eyes'?[7] It will come back to you, depend on that; and you will remember, then, that your son cursed you for the love of his mother. I am going now. You will not see me more, and I hope I may never see you again, either in this world or the next."

He was about to rush from the house, but his sister prevented him. "Gillie," she cried, "you will not go without bidding me good-bye?"

"No, Maddy, and Mumsey, too," he said, returning to embrace them; "I shall never forget your love to me; never—never!"

"But you will come back, my dear boy. You cannot go like this," said Ethel.

"Never, whilst that man lives," replied the lad, determinedly.

"But you have no money, no clothes."

"I will write to you; you can send them to me," he said.

"That she certainly will not do," said the Professor, as he drew his wife away. "If you leave this house, sir, you leave it forever, and will never have any assistance from me as long as you live."

"All right; I don't want it," cried Gilbert, as he ran out of the house, and slammed the hall door after him.

"It is impossible. You cannot let him go like this," said Ethel, indignantly.

"He has made it possible for himself," replied the Professor.

---

[7] Luke chpt 16, v. 23: 'And in hell he lift up his eyes, being in torments, and seeth Abraham afar off, and Lazarus in his bosom.

"He has chosen to rebel against my authority, and, with my consent, he never enters these doors again."

He turned away to the library as he spoke, leaving the two women to gaze at each other aghast, and wonder what was to happen next.

- CHAPTER TWO -

A PLEASANT EVENING

After this scene, the dinner party was hardly likely to be a success, at all events, for Ethel Aldwyn. She looked very pretty in the plain, black dress she chose to wear, which was just cut down at the neck to show her fair white throat, nestled in billows of soft lace. She arranged her hair very carefully, and tried hard to erase the traces of emotion from her countenance; but her eyelids were red and swollen from weeping, and her lips quivered as she spoke. Maddy had gone up to bed, utterly refusing to take anything to eat or drink. She was much attached to her brother Gilbert, and declared, vehemently, that if he did not return home, she should follow him. Her step-mother had been arguing the matter with her, and begging her to do nothing rash or hasty. She had a secret dread in her heart regarding Madeline, which she had never mentioned, even to the girl herself.

The year before, she had been thrown into contact with the family of one of her school companions, and, though they had not been quite of her own social standing, Ethel had not liked to discourage the intimacy, because the Reynolds had been very kind to Maddy, and the girl had few young friends, on account of her father never allowing her to invite any girls to visit her at her own home. Her step-mother had felt glad at first, therefore, to see the interest she took in going to the Reynolds' house, until she found out, by accident, that the eldest son was carrying on a sort of flirtation with Madeline. Wilfred Reynolds was a handsome, smart, young fellow, but very commonplace; and Ethel knew well that the Professor—who, notwithstanding his unamiable disposition, was undeniably a gentleman by birth—would never consent to an engagement, or marriage, between his daughter and the Reynolds' son. She had, therefore, tried to lessen the intimacy by every means in her power; but she had not been entirely successful; and, when

14

Maddy talked about leaving home, or having her revenge, she was always afraid she entertained some idea of eloping with young Mr. Reynolds. She did not like the dogged manner with which Maddy had received the episode of the afternoon. The girl was very high-spirited, and capable of taking strong measures in order to get her own way. Ethel dreaded the effect of Gilbert's quarrel with his father upon her nature, which was not unlike the Professor's in its obstinacy and high temper. She felt very uneasy about both her step-children, and descended to the drawing-room, to receive her guests, in anything but a happy mood.

Mr. Bunster and Mr. Robson were too partial to a good dinner to have refused the invitation; and they were both standing on the hearth-rug, arrayed in white waistcoats and swallow-tailed coats,[8] when she entered the room. The Professor was with them, talking as amicably on the topics of the day, as if he had had no disturbance in the house, and his only son was comfortably domesticated beneath the paternal roof. His pale-blue eyes did not show the least trace of emotion, nor his manner annoyance. He was absorbed in the discussion of some new book, and did not even lift his eyes when his young wife came up to his side. He did just raise them, as Mr. Bunster officiously questioned her as to whether she had not caught a cold in the rough weather they had been having—her eyes looked just a little inflamed to him—but, after one glance of caution, he dropped them again, and returned to his argument.

The dinner had been announced, and the party was about to adjourn to the dining-room, when a slight commotion was heard in the hall. Ethel started. Could it be Gilbert come back again, finding out already, perhaps, how hopeless opposition to home authority is, when one has no other resources?—when her ear caught the sound of a familiar voice, and her face flushed crimson.

"Who can that be demanding admittance at this hour?" asked Professor Aldwyn. "James! say we are engaged, and can see no one."

"O! no, you don't," cried a merry voice, through the open door;

---

[8] An evening dress-coat with two long tapering tails at the back.

"for I've come expressly to dine with my cousin Ethel!" and, at the same moment, Captain Edward Standish, of the steamship "Davenport," entered the room, and grasped Mrs. Aldwyn by the hand.

"Why, my dear Ethel, am I late?" he exclaimed. "I thought your dinner-hour was half-past seven. You expected me, of course. Why, how strange you look. Surely, you are not ill? And aren't you glad to see me?"

"Yes, Ned, very glad," stammered Ethel; "only—only—I thought—"

"What did you think, my dear?"

"*I* will answer that question, sir," interposed the Professor. "Your cousin thought, after the wire she sent you this morning, that you would delay giving us the pleasure of your company until you heard from us again."

"*Did* you send me a wire, Ethel?" exclaimed Captain Standish, with surprise. "Well, I've not been back to my hotel since the morning—had my things sent on to the club—so I never got the message. But, bless you!" he went on in his jolly fashion, "I should have come all the same, wire or not; for I have to go back to Plymouth the day after to-morrow, and I meant to see you before I sailed again. How are you, Professor? Jolly, eh? You don't get fatter, do you? You should take a voyage with me. That would make another man of you. What! is dinner ready? Come along, Ethel. I shall take you in myself. O, yes, I daresay I'm the most unworthy individual present, but I take precedence as a blood relation; so, no excuse. Wait till dinner is over," he continued, as they moved towards the dining-room, "and you shall see what you shall see. I've got the loveliest things for you and Maddy, from Japan. By the way, where is Maddy? Not absent from home, I hope?"

"Oh, no," replied Mrs. Aldwyn, hesitatingly; "but you will not see her to-night, Ned. She has a headache, and has gone to bed."

"Poor girl! Well, I'm lucky to have found you. And fancy your sending a wire to put me off. You nasty little thing."

"I—we—that is, the Professor thought," she answered, unwillingly, "that, as he had some scientific friends coming to-night, you would rather visit us some other time, Ned. But it doesn't signify, of course. You know how welcome you are."

"Of course I do! Weren't we brought up together from babies; and do you suppose, for a moment, I would let anything come between us. Here, let me carve that lamb for you; I'm a regular dab at carving. I have to do it at the saloon-table, you know."

"Bring that lamb to me," said the Professor, in a severe tone, to the man servant. "If Mrs. Aldwyn is unequal to so simple a task, *I* am the proper person to undertake it."

"O! of course you are. Wish you joy of it. Only I wanted to make myself useful," said Captain Standish with open eyes.

After this little episode, the Professor seemed to try to make himself purposely offensive to his latest guest. He preserved a dead silence when the Captain told any of his sea stories, or perpetrated some innocent little joke; and it was evident to the whole party that his presence was unwelcome to the host. At last, when the dessert was over, Professor Aldwyn rose, and, telling his wife to have coffee served in the library for himself and his friends, said:

"Come, Bunster and Robson, let us go where we may have some peace. It is impossible to discuss any sensible matter with a hubbub like this going on.

And, without a word of apology to his wife, or Captain Standish, he stalked from the room, followed by his own friends.

Ned Standish looked at Ethel, with a comical glance of dismay.

"What's up? What is the matter? Have I done or said anything wrong?"

"O! no, no!" replied his cousin, who was ready to cry. "It has nothing to do with you, Ned. The Professor is rather queer, sometimes, you know, and only fit company for himself and his cronies. And he has had a good deal to upset him to-day. His son and he have had a serious quarrel, which has made us all miserable. Gilbert has left the house, declaring he will never return to it; and we don't know where he has gone, nor what he will do, so we are all uneasy. Pray, think no more of the Professor's manner. He was never a courtier, you know."

Ned Standish looked her narrowly in the face. He seemed as though he would have said something sympathetic, but was afraid to trust himself. So he jumped up from the table, instead, and exclaimed, in a brisk voice:

"Well, never mind him. He is happy now, with his cronies. Let us be happy, too. Come into the drawing-room, and let me prove to you that I have not forgotten my old playfellow during my wanderings."

He went into the hall, and pulled a large parcel after him into the drawing-room, where he immediately commenced to unpack it. Ethel called out with delight, as its contents were displayed to view.

"O how I wish Maddy was here," she exclaimed, with girlish pleasure, as Captain Standish produced roll after roll of soft, white Japanese gauze, and pale tinted silks, quaintly carved silver trays and boxes, painted fans, and all sorts of curious toys, in the shape of huge beetles and frogs and butterflies, finishing up with a beautifully inlaid cabinet, of great value, for her especial acceptance.

"O Ned, Ned! did you really get all these for us? How very good of you. I thought you had forgotten me long ago."

"Forgotten you, Ethel?" he answered, with a strange softness in his voice, "*Never!* I shall never forget you, nor the happy days we spent in Beer,[9] as long as I live."

"O don't speak of Beer," she cried. "Ned, I have never been home once since my marriage. The Professor says it is childish of me to want to do so. But I dream of it, oh, so often, and long to see the dear, old place, with its honeysuckles and roses blooming all the winter, down in sweet Devonshire."

"But, why won't he let you go? You should assert your dignity, Ethel, and insist upon it. Your father and mother must be longing to see you again."

"O, yes; they are. And they came up to London last year to visit me; but you see how it is, Ned, he doesn't like visitors. They disturb him at his studies, and I don't think father and mother felt very comfortable. The Professor is so much cleverer than any of us. I am afraid we are not suitable company for him."

---

[9] Beer – a seaside village in east Devon which was very popular with smugglers in the eighteenth and nineteenth centuries. A Miss Jane Bidney of Beer made the lace trim for Queen Victoria's wedding dress in 1839.

"And yet you married him, Ethel," said Captain Standish, curiously.

"Ah! Ned, don't speak of it. It is best not mentioned. Let me look at these beautiful things, instead, and be happy in thinking how kindly my cousin has thought of me in absence."

"And that he will always be your friend. Remember that, also, Ethel. But I am afraid, my poor girl, that you are not, you cannot be, happy."

"Hush, Ned! No one is quite happy in this world, you know, and, I daresay, my lot is as good as that of most. I shall keep all my treasures in this lovely little cabinet. How exquisitely these birds are inlaid, and the pink flowers. What are they?"

"They are the blossoms of the almond tree, which grows in profusion in Japan. The whole country is rosy with them in their season. But, Ethel," looking at his watch, "it is past ten o'clock. I think I had better be making a start. I have so many things to do before joining my ship, that I don't want to be late out of bed. I shall not disturb the Professor again. He will not break his heart because he has missed the opportunity of wishing me good-by. So, farewell, my dear little cousin. Keep up your heart; and, if you ever find yourself in any difficulty out of which I can help you, my agents, Harwood & Crowe, will always forward a letter to me wherever I may be. Good-by, God bless you!" and he wrung Ethel's hand heartily.

As soon as he was gone, the poor girl sat down beside the presents he had brought her, and cried as if her heart would break. He had reminded her so powerfully of her home and all the dear ones she had left there. Three or four years before, she and cousin Ned had been engaged to be married. But a silly quarrel about some other girl had taken place between them, and he had gone back to sea before they had made it up again. So they had drifted apart, and Ethel had considered herself free. Professor Aldwyn had come down to Beer, which is on the seacoast, with his children, for change of air; and she had married him chiefly for the reason that most women marry: because he had proposed to her, and no other eligible man was present to take the shine out of him. Her parents had thought it would be an excellent match for her. The

Professor had been on his best behaviour. Ethel had made great friends with his children, and fancied she could be quite happy passing her life with them. And so the mistake had come to pass, as so many other mistakes have done before it. She sat for two or three hours alone, examining and admiring the gifts which her cousin had brought her, inhaling the strange, sweet perfume which pervaded them, and handling the soft silks and gauzes, as she fabricated dresses and tea-gowns out of them for herself and Maddy, in her mind's eye.

At last, she heard the library door open and shut, and footsteps sounded in the hall. Messrs. Bunster and Robson had finished their discussion, and were about to return home. After the last few words had been spoken, the hall door shut, and the Professor entered the drawing-room, and took up his station on the hearth-rug. His wife noted, with secret alarm, that he was still displeased with her, and prepared for a lecture.

"Where did you get all that rubbish?" he commenced, as he surveyed the dress pieces and toys with which the tables were covered.

"My cousin brought them for me," she answered, quietly.

"I won't have them in the room. Throw them all out," said the Professor.

"What harm do they do?" she expostulated. "I shall take them up-stairs presently."

"Throw them out into the passage, at once, I say. If you don't do it, I will chuck them out myself." And, suiting the action to the word, he dealt a violent kick at the inlaid cabinet, which broke in its panelled side.

"O, Henry! my cabinet! You have ruined it," cried Ethel. "How cruel you are to me. Why should you have done that? And it must have cost ever so much money. Ned brought it all the way from Japan, expressly for me."

"Ned! Ned! Ned!" repeated the Professor, in a tone which was intended to imitate her own. "And, pray, why did you not obey my orders with regard to 'Ned'? I told you to send a wire to tell him not to come here this evening."

"And so I did. I sent it at once."

"I don't believe it. You are lying to me. You heard the fellow say, himself, that he had never received it."

"I have never lied to you, Henry. It is most unjust of you to say so. I wanted to see my cousin very much, but I sent the telegram just the same; and it was quite as great a surprise to me as to you, when he came in."

"I don't believe you, madam. I saw how particular you were in dressing yourself this evening. A new dress, with roses in your bosom! Roses, indeed, in March!"

"It was *not* a new dress," said his wife, indignantly. "It is quite an old one, which I had freshened up with some clean lace. And, as for the roses, Mrs. Vernon gave them to me out of her conservatory, yesterday."

"That is easily enough said," sneered the Professor. "The fact remains that you deceived me with regard to the telegram, and that you were determined to receive that man, whether I would or not. But it is the last time. You receive no more of your lovers in my house."

"My lovers!" exclaimed Ethel, flushing scarlet. "How *dare* you say so."

"Was not Captain Edward Standish your lover, before you did me the honour to marry me?"

"No; our engagement had been broken off years before. Indeed, it scarcely could be called an engagement, I was such a child. It was only a cousinly flirtation, and you know it well enough."

"I know that you shall never see the man again, with my permission; and, if he forces his way into the house, as he did to-night, I will tell my servants to kick him out."

"It would be worthy of you," she answered; "but you may be sure that neither he, nor any of my relations, shall enter your house to be insulted. They are far too good for that."

"O, that is your opinion, is it? Well, then, I beg that Captain Standish's love offerings may follow his example, and make their exit for the last time."

And, throwing up a window, the Professor commenced to throw the bales of silk and muslin out of it into the London street. Ethel stood by and watched him without making a remonstrance.

She knew it would be useless, and that her entreaties to be allowed to retain them would only result in more abuse being heaped upon her head. But, as the last treasure met its fate, and she heard the Japanese cabinet fall with a crash upon the pavement below, she drew herself up to her full height, and said, slowly:

"O, you are a hard, cruel man. Gilbert was right when he said, to-day, that God would bring it home to you. Have you ever thought of any one but yourself, lived for any one but yourself, in this life yet? How happy your first wife was to go so soon. How I wish that I could follow her. But the day will come, Henry, when you will look round you for affection, and find none. Mark my words! You have never tried to win the love of any one whilst you lived; and, when you die, there will not be one honest tear shed over your grave."

It was the worst thing she had ever said to him yet; but he did not feel it. Such men do not feel whilst they remain on this earth. Professor Aldwyn had suffered the selfish nature, which prompted him to live for himself and his own pleasures alone, to gain so much the mastery over him, that he did not recognize it as such. He only thought that the whole world (and, especially, his particular part of it) was set up in opposition to his wishes; and was determined that his wife and children, at least, should comply with them. He turned, grandly, to where poor Ethel stood, with her moist eyes and flushed cheeks, and said:

"Leave the room, and do not enter my presence again until you have learned how to behave yourself."

"I am willing enough to do that, Henry; but I must tell you what I think, first. You have driven your only son from your house, and anything that may befall him will lie at your door. If Gilbert goes wrong, or meets with some terrible death, it will be accounted to you as surely as if you had killed him, or led him astray. He is your child; you are accountable to God for him; and if he errs, as err he must, poor boy, cast on the world at his tender age, *you* will have to work out the penalty of his wrong-doing. I entreat you to think of it, before it is too late, and he has gone too far to be recalled. It is not only Gilbert; Maddy is as likely to run away from home as he. She loves her brother, dearly; and your harshness to him has sunk deeply into her soul. I cannot be responsible for her, if you stand aloof and will not do your share of the duty."

"Anything more?" demanded the Professor, sternly.

"Only to believe what I tell you," replied Ethel. "That I am perfectly innocent of displeasing you intentionally; that I *did* send that telegram, and had no idea that my cousin would come here to-night."

"And I repeat that it is a falsehood; and I would not believe you if you swore it till you were black in the face. If my daughter is going wrong (as you seem to indicate), she will owe it to your example. A woman who can wish to hold any communication, after she is married, with a former lover, must have a degraded nature, and is not fit to have the charge of an innocent girl."

"I do not wish to have the charge of her; I will not keep it," cried Ethel, passionately, "if you continue to insult me like this. Let me go back to my own people. Better a crust with them than this life of suspicion and distrust."

"Your own people," sneered the Professor. "Why not say your own *cousin*, at once? That's the fellow you're hankering after. Do you suppose I can't see it? And you'd like to run after him, wouldn't you, and tell him how you've been ill-treated here, and ask him to comfort you, eh?"

"I shall answer you no more," replied his wife, as she prepared to leave the room. "Why was I ever such a fool as to imagine a man, who refused to go to his father when he lay dying, would have sufficient heart to make either a good parent to his own children, or a generous husband to the unfortunate women who were foolish enough to marry him?"

And with that, Mrs. Aldwyn walked up to her own room, leaving the Professor looking rather foolish. She had hit him on a sore point. If there was one incident in his selfish life which he regretted, it was the fact that he had not been present at his old father's death-bed. His father had been good and generous to him, and he was, perhaps, the person for whom he had felt the utmost affection of which his cold-blooded nature was capable. But he had been employed on some very interesting and difficult scientific experiments when summoned to his sick-bed, and he had delayed going until it was too late; till the good, old man had passed away, saying, to the very last moment, "Henry might have come." There was nothing Professor Aldwyn liked to be reminded of less than this; and, as his wife left him, he walked back to his library and sat down in his large arm-chair. The fire was still smouldering on the hearth, and the room felt warm. He thought he would sit there for a little and compose himself. He did not care to join Ethel again so soon; and the events of the day seemed to have upset him a little. He felt unusually languid and sleepy, and yet he did not feel inclined to rest. His heart had always suffered from slow circulation, and, at times, he had been warned against excitement or hurry. He knew what did him good on such occasions—a strong glass of whiskey or brandy. The liquor case stood on the table beside him, and he filled a bumper and drank it off. Suspicious and reserved by nature, he credited others with his own failings, and really believed that Ethel had deceived him with regard to Captain Standish. That idea was not calculated to do his heart any good; but the allusion to his father had had a far worse effect upon him. The lamps had been lowered, and he was sitting there by the light of the fire, alone; and, as it flickered lower and lower, he was foolish enough to fancy that he saw the form of his old father standing at the opposite side of the table to him. He rubbed his eyes, and gazed at the figure steadfastly; but it still stood there, looking at him earnestly, as it appeared, but very gravely, in order to dispel so absurd a fancy, the Professor closed his eyes, as though in sleep. He felt a strange sort of faintness steal over him, not painful, but very unusual, as if he were sinking down through the chair cushions to the very floor. He believed that sleep was really stealing over him, and yielded himself up to its influence. His eyes remained closed; his head sunk further and further back on the crimson-plush bolster, until he lost all consciousness—and slept, indeed.

- CHAPTER THREE -

THE PROFESSOR BEGINS TO LIVE

How long the Professor remained unconscious to external things, he could not have said; but, when he awoke again, he found himself standing at the back of the chair in which he had fallen asleep, holding on to it with his two hands. He felt strangely giddy and weak, as if he had just emerged from a long illness; and, for a while, he could not collect his thoughts, nor realize where he was. But, as his swaying figure somewhat steadied itself, and his senses returned to him, he knew that he was grasping the back of his own armchair.

"This is really very strange," he thought; "how ever did I get here? Surely, I fell asleep in this chair. I must have walked in my sleep."

His hands wandered about the soft-cushioned velvet, as he spoke to himself, until they rested on the top of a man's head—the head of a man, who, apparently, still occupied the seat he had vacated. The Professor started. Who could it be? Who had had the impudence to enter his private room and usurp his seat? Did it mean robbery, or bloodshed, or violence of some sort? He was a nervous man, and he was conscious he had more enemies than friends in the world.

The room was now sunk in profound darkness. The fire had completely died out, and the atmosphere was intensely cold. And yet, it did not strike the Professor as strange that he could see all the objects in it. The touch of the stranger's head had made him shudder with apprehension; but he felt compelled to see who he was. and defend himself against him, if necessary. He seized a wooden ruler off his writing-table, and crept cautiously round to the front of the arm-chair. How very strange and uncertain his limbs felt as he did so! For a moment, the question flashed through his mind if he had not exceeded a little, when drinking with his friends the night before. As a rule, he was a most abstemious man; but he had been rather put out on this occasion, and may have taken more champagne than was good for him. And then, the glass of brandy he had swallowed afterwards; surely, the liquor must have had an effect on him; he could account in no other way for the very unusual sensations he experienced. He had been moving slowly round the table, as he pondered after this fashion, grasping the ruler in his hand, determined to see who it was that had dared to invade his privacy. He had reached the front of the arm-chair by this time, and stood upon the hearth-rug. He was in full view of the man who slept in his favourite seat, and he gazed at him aghast—it was *himself!*

"Good God!" exclaimed the Professor, as the truth burst on him. But there was no doubt of it. There he lay, stretched out most comfortably, in the dress suit in which he had spent the evening, with the empty glass, in which he had drank the brandy, on the table beside him, with his hands folded on his chest, and his eyes fast shut. He looked very calm and peaceful, as if he had suffered no pain; but he was unmistakably Professor Aldwyn, or, rather, what had been he. The Professor put out his finger timidly, and touched the dead body on the forehead. It was cold as ice. There was no question about it. The spirit had departed from it.

"But, good God!" again exclaimed the Professor; "who then am I?" Then the great truth flashed across his mind.

"Is it possible? Can it really be the case? Have I passed out of my body? Is my connection with earth broken forever?"

He glanced up as he thought thus, and again saw standing, on the opposite side of the table, the figure of his old father, who solemnly bowed an affirmative answer to his questioning.

"Father," exclaimed the Professor, relieved to recognize some one who could explain the mystery to him, "tell me, am I right, and is this Death?"

His father bowed again.

"Come nearer," cried the Professor; "take my hand. Let me feel, in this crisis of nature, that I have some one to support and strengthen me."

But his father's spirit faded away, without a response. Suddenly, the whole story of his own defalcation, when the old man had yearned to see his son on his deathbed, and he never went near him, flashed on the Professor's memory; and a voice seemed to murmur in his ear, "It shall be meted unto you again."

A sickening horror of the whole business took possession of him, as if the body, lying in the arm-chair, were not his own, but that of some one else. He tried to move further away from it; to go to the other end of the library, where was placed a large, luxurious couch; but he found he was unable to do so. Some invisible, but powerful attraction, chained him to the vicinity of the corpse, and he was forced to remain where he was, gazing at it.

"But how can this be?" he thought. "What have I always heard and been taught, that people, as soon as they die, are taken away, either to heaven or hell! If I am dead (which I certainly do not feel like), why am I still here? Why have I not been carried away to another world? Why have I not wings, or—or—the other thing? I don't understand it. I must be dreaming. I am suffering from nightmare, and will wake presently and laugh at my imaginary distress. It is impossible it can be true, and I still remaining in the library at home. It would be too utterly absurd."

He stood there, gazing at the quiet sleeper in the arm-chair for some time longer, wishing that the dream would end and he could wake up again.

"I was a fool to go to sleep in a chair," he mused. "It always has some unpleasant effect. I should have gone straight up to bed at once." But, at this juncture, his meditations were interrupted by the entrance of the housemaid, who bounced into the room noisily, and, going straight up to the windows, threw back the shutters, and let the March daylight into the apartment. The Professor, although fully clothed, as far as he was aware, felt a strange shyness before the maid servant, and said some words of explanation, with regard to her finding him there at such an unusual hour, which she did not seem to hear. But as she turned from the window to take up the hearth-rug, and perceived the silent figure in the arm-chair, she gave a fell shriek, and rushed out of the room again.

"This is very strange," thought the Professor, "can this really be a nightmare? Why did Mary not see me? I called her by name. Why did she not hear my voice? I begin to think I must be ill. I am in a fever and delirious. But I never felt better in my life. It is all very strange amid inexplicable."

But here appeared the faces of James, the footman, and Sarah, the cook, at the open door, whilst behind them came Mary; all with expressions of the greatest alarm.

"Don't be afraid," the Professor said to them; "I am only suffering from nightmare. It will be over in a minute. Come here and wake me, James, as you are used to do in the mornings."

But no one of them heeded him.

"O, poor master," exclaimed the cook; "whatever will the missus say?"

"La, cook, don't let's go a step nearer," said Mary. "He do look awful; you can't think. I shall never get over the fright all my life long."

"Now, don't talk nonsense," interposed the more heroic James. "I daresay it's only a fit he's in. Or maybe he's had a drop too much. You females are always for making a scare. Why, he's lying there as natural as possible, from what I can see. No more dead than I am, I'll lay you tuppence."

"You jist go round and look at his face," said the housemaid. "You won't talk about scares then. If he ain't dead, poor feller, well I've never seen a dead 'un, that's all. I nearly died myself when I seen 'im."

"Lor', gals, and so he is, sure enough," said James, as he came round to the hearth-rug and looked the corpse in the face. "Dead as a door nail. What a sudden thing. He must have gone off in a fit-like. Well, to be sure. Pore master. He was a bad 'un, if ever there was such; but we mustn't remember it against 'im, now he's dead and gone."

Here Sarah approached, timidly, and touched the body.

"Lauks, he's as cold as cold. He must have been gone for hours. My, James, do give me a drop of that brandy, for it makes me feel quite faint-like. What are we to do about it?"

"What o'clock is it?" said the footman, glancing at the time-piece, "seven o'clock, and he's bin here the best part of the night. Now, the fust thing is to fetch the doctor, or we may get into a scrape. So, you two gals go down to the kitchen, and keep as quiet as you can. Don't you let the missus know, whatever you do; the doctor will do that part of the business; and if you'll clear out I'll lock the door, and fetch Doctor Barnes as quick as I can."

"Aye," remarked the cook, significantly, as they hustled out of the room. "He wouldn't let the young missus call in Doctor Barnes, when she had such terrible pain last week; but he little thought, the next time he was fetched, 'twould be to look at his corpus. He's been real hard on her at times; God forgive him."

"That he have," acquiesced Mary. "I wonder how she'll take it."

"*I* don't," replied James.

"And that pore lad, too; gone only yesterday, and wandering about, the Lord only knows where. It do seem like a judgment, now, don't it?"

And with that the Professor heard them carefully close the door, and lock it on the outside.

It was not a nightmare, then; he actually was dead. Well, it was the most curious thing that had ever occurred to him. Where was hell, and where was heaven? Should he never be able to get away from that room? What was the matter with him, that he could not fly? This was totally opposite from everything that he had ever been told of the change called death. In an incredibly short time, as it seemed to him, Doctor Barnes entered the room, with James, on tiptoe, and came tip to his side. He spoke to him; he even pulled him by the sleeve, or appeared to do so; but the doctor took no notice of the appeal. He went, straight up to the corpse, pulled open the eyelids placed his hand over the bosom, and then said, briefly:

"Failure of the action of the heart. Been dead for hours; probably seven. How comes he to be in evening clothes?"

"We had a dinner party last night, sir," replied the servant.

"Ah! excited himself, did he?"

"I don't know, sir. The master sat up after we had gone to bed. I didn't know but what he was in bed, as usual, till Mary come in this morning and gave the alarm. He must have come back to the libery after the gentlemen as dined here was gone."

"Ah! any trouble yesterday that you know of?"

"Master Gilbert and the master, they had a terrible quarrel, sir, about two o'clock, which no one couldn't help hearing. A regular fight, as you may say, sir; and the young gentleman, he ran out of the house, and haven't been back since."

"That did the mischief, doubtless," said Doctor Barnes. "I've warned the Professor again and again against any violent excitement; but he has not heeded me. Well, the body cannot remain thus. I must go and break the sad news to Mrs. Aldwyn. Tell one of the maids to say that the Professor is not very well, and that I wish to speak to her. Meanwhile, I will lock this door again, and write a certificate of death."

As the two men left the room, the Professor could not help thinking to himself what an ungrateful crew they were. James had been in his service over two years, and had not only received handsome wages for his trouble, but been the recipient of all his cast-off clothes. Dr. Barnes, too, had eaten many and many a dinner at his expense, besides having had his bills settled regularly every Christmas. But neither of them had said a good word for him, or expressed a regret that he was gone. All they thought of was how his wife would take the announcement of his demise, and what formalities were to be gone through in connection with it. He remembered that he had left the doctor ten pounds, in his will, to purchase a mourning ring,[10] and he felt sorry for it. He wanted very much to accompany them, and witness how his wife and daughter took the news which they had to tell them. But, notwithstanding every endeavour, he could not detach himself from his cast-off body. He could not shake himself free of it. It seemed to cling to him like the Old Man of the Sea to Sindbad.[11]

Ethel Aldwyn had passed a sleepless night. The interview she had had with the Professor, just before retiring to rest, had made

[10] Mourning rings were just one item amongst many types of mourning-jewellery in the nineteenth century. They often contained hair from the deceased or could be set with black enamel, jet, diamonds, pearls or miniature portraits.
[11] This is a reference to the Arabian Nights and the fifth voyage of Sinbad the Sailor. The Old Man of the Sea begs Sinbad to carry him across a brook but then refuses to get down from Sinbad's shoulders. After many days Sinbad only manages to remove the old man by getting him drunk so that he falls off.

her heart beat so fast, and, altogether, produced so much agitation in her frame, that all desire to sleep seemed to have been banished from her eyes. She was nervous, and frightened, in the bargain; she dreaded a renewal of the warfare as soon as her husband should join her; so she had lain awake, listening for his footstep on the stairs, till she worked herself into a state of agitation. When she found that he did not come, she became more nervous still. That betokened that he was so angry he refused to speak to her again. Perhaps he meant to take her at her word, and send her home to her parents at Beer, as soon as day dawned. She longed to see her old home, poor girl; and she would have been happier than she dared say, if she could have thought she would never have seen her husband again. Still, the idea, however welcome, was too novel not to be perplexing, and she could not rest in consequence. The message that Mary brought her, with a very mysterious face—that Doctor Barnes wanted to see her, because the Professor was not at all well—conveyed no notion whatever of the truth to her mind. Professor Aldwyn had been used to consider himself very ill at times, though he never could be brought to think any one else so. She believed their dispute of the night before must have had something to do with his sending for the doctor; but she jumped out of bed quickly enough when she heard it.

"Not *really* ill, surely, Mary!" she exclaimed. "And what can Doctor Barnes want to see me about it for, when, as you know, the master will never let any one touch his medicines but himself?"

"That was the message I was ordered to give you, if you please, ma'am," replied the maid, primly, as if she would say: "I could tell you a deal more if I might"— "And I do think the master is worse than usual; and, the doctor, he think badly of him."

Ethel turned pale.

"O, Mary, you don't say so? Give me my stockings and shoes; there's a good girl; and get my tea-gown out of the wardrobe. I must run down just as I am. The doctor will excuse me. Where is he? In the library?"

"No, ma'am," replied the girl, with a shudder; "he is in your boo-dore."

The boudoir was next the bedroom; and, in another minute,

Ethel was in the presence of Doctor Barnes.

"Doctor!" she cried; "do tell me at once. What is the matter with my husband? Where is he? Why have you not brought him up to his own room?"

"He is coming up, directly, my dear Mrs. Aldwyn," returned the doctor; "that is, if you will compose yourself. I have bad news for you; but you must try and bear it bravely."

"Bad news!" repeated Ethel.

"Yes; I have told you before that the Professor's heart action was not entirely satisfactory, and that it behooved him to be careful of excitement or worry, have I not?"

"Yes," faltered Ethel; "but is it *I* who have worried him, doctor?"

"*You*, my dear child," said the doctor, paternally. "Why, what put such an idea into your head? No; certainly not. But I understand from your servants that there was a disturbance here yesterday, before Master Gilbert left home."

"O, yes, doctor; a sad disturbance. They quarrelled, and that, necessarily, upset my husband. Is that the cause of his illness?"

"I am afraid it must have had a bad effect upon the Professor, the action of the heart being so slow; and so—"

"But how was he taken ill?" asked Mrs. Aldwyn. "Shall I go to him, Doctor Barnes? Does he want me?"

"No, Mrs. Aldwyn; he does not want you. He will never want you on earth again. Do you understand me?"

A frightened look came into her eyes.

"You mean—O! surely not!—that—that—he—"

"Yes; you have guessed it. I mean that he has gone beyond our assistance—that he is dead. Don't excite yourself, pray," said the doctor, who had a horror of feminine hysterics. "Don't scream. It can do him no good; but try to be thankful that he has died without pain."

"Are you quite sure of that?" asked Ethel.

"Quite sure. His death was due to failure of the action of the heart. He must have died in his sleep, or nearly so. I have anticipated such an end for him for some time past. Now, will you take my advice and return to your own room, whilst we bring the body

32

up-stairs?"

She turned from him without another word, and re-entered her bedroom. But when she found herself alone, with the door locked behind her, she burst into a natural flood of weeping, during which she kept on murmuring to herself: "O, poor Henry! *poor* Henry! To be called away so suddenly, without any preparation; and when his last words to Gilbert were so cruel and unkind. God forgive him. And I was angry with him, too. May God forgive me, also. I wouldn't have spoken to him as I did, if I had known it would so soon be over. Poor Henry! How little love he gained for himself during this life!"

- CHAPTER FOUR -

WHAT THEY THOUGHT OF HIM

A s soon as the doctor had time to think calmly, he decided that it would be better to leave the Professor's body in the library, until it was carried to the grave.

"Why should that poor, young creature up-stairs be made more nervous than necessary? Besides, if she elects to remain in this house, her bedroom will be full of unpleasant memories. No, it will be quite easy to lay the body out here on the long table, and let it be taken hence to the cemetery. James, I will go home now, and send some one, at once, to do all that is necessary for your poor master. Meanwhile, you must keep the key of the room yourself, and take care that no one, especially your mistress, gets access to it. When everything is arranged decently, and in order, you can take the key to Mrs. Aldwyn, and tell her what we have done. I will return this afternoon, and ascertain her wishes about the funeral. Is there any one, you know of, to whom I should telegraph on behalf of your mistress, or the late Professor?"

"Missus, she has plenty of friends," replied the man. "Her people, they live down at Beer, in Devonshire; but as for 'im," indicating the corpse, with a backward-cast thumb, "I don't believe there's many as would care the one way or the other."

"Ah, perhaps not," remarked the doctor. "But Mrs. Aldwyn is too young to be left alone at such a time; so I shall wire the news to her father and mother, and then they can do as they choose. Here is the key. Now, mind you are careful of the directions I have given you."

The servant promised, and the doctor departed.

When the loquacious old women arrived to pull and turn about his body; to undress it, wash it, put on it a clean night-shirt, stretch it out on a board laid on the library table, and envelop it in a sheet, the Professor was keenly conscious of the whole proceedings. He did his very best to sever the invisible links that bound him to his dead self, and which compelled him to listen to every word that was interchanged with James or Sarah. But all in vain. It seemed as though a cord of iron bound him to the corpse, and forced him to hear all the unkind things people were saying of him, now that he was gone.

"Well, he is as plain a body as ever I see," said one old hag, as she washed his face and dried it with a rough towel. "I wonder what the pretty, young lady up-stairs was thinking of when she threw herself away on such as he. 'Ideous, I calls 'im, with that sandy hair, and motley complexion."

"Ah, but he was very clever, you see," quoth James. "A scientist, as they calls it; and clever people ain't 'ansome, as a rule, you know."

"O, fiddle," exclaimed the other lady, irreverently.

"Don't yer tell me. Brains ain't got nothing to do with noses. But I suppose 'e was awful rich. That's what the gals marries for mostly, now-a-days."

"Ah, well," said James, confidentially, "it's early times to say much; but I don't s'pose as she'll miss him, nor find no difficulty in getting some one to fill 'is place; twiggez-vous?"

"Lor', Mr. James, you are allays so funny-like. But 'tis 'ard for a woman to go through life alone; so, who's to blame 'er? I am sure if 'e had been my lot, I should have got a better-looking one, as soon as I had the chance."

"Old brute," thought the Professor. Indeed, he said it; but no sound broke the stillness of the air. The women, having completed their gruesome task, tied up his chin with a white handkerchief, making him look just like an old woman; and, having placed two pennies on his eyelids to keep them closed, they pulled down the blinds, tidied the room, and walked away on tip-toe, in case they met any of the members of the family. The Professor looked round him in dismay. For how long was he to remain a prisoner there? Was he condemned, throughout eternity, to walk, or lie, or sit beside this wretched carcass, for which he had no further use? He retained all his senses, his brains, eyesight, hearing, and feeling. Why could he not use them? If this was what had been described to him as "the other world," he would rather be resolved into dust with the body he saw before him. How time went, he had no idea; but some hours later, perhaps, he heard the key again turn in the lock; this time very slowly, and uncertainly, and then, after a pause, as though the visitor hacked the courage to enter, light footsteps crossed the threshold, the owner of which was expostulating with some one who was trying to drag her backwards.

"Come, dear Maddy, be brave. Why, what is there to be frightened of? Do you suppose poor papa would harm you, even if it were possible for him to do so?"

"No, no; it is not that. Don't think me so foolish. But, oh, Mumsey, darling, I don't want to look at him. It is very wicked of me, I know; but I cannot forget dear Gilbert, out in all this wretched weather, friendless and alone, without money, and without a home. And when I think of it, I feel I cannot enter this room as I ought."

"My, dear, do you mean to say you cannot forgive poor papa, even now?"

"No, I can't; and if I said otherwise I should tell a lie. What difference can his death make? Can it bring back Gilbert to us?"

"Yes, dearest; it can, and it shall," replied Ethel, as she kissed her step-daughter. "It was the first thing I thought of; you may be sure of that. I have wired to my solicitor to set inquiries on foot at once; and kind old Doctor Barnes has promised to assist us all in his power. Cheer up, dear Maddy. We shall have Gilbert home again, I hope, before the funeral takes place."

"This is pleasant," thought the Professor; "that rebellious boy, who actually slapped me in the face, is to be reinstated, with due honour, in order to follow me with appropriate rejoicings, I suppose, to my last home. O if I could only get into my body again, what a disappointment I would give them all."

He was so close to the corpse that, as his wife approached it, he could touch her.

As Ethel, unconsciously, felt his spiritual presence, she shuddered. "How very cold it is," she said; "I wonder if Doctor Barnes ordered them to leave the windows open. Courage, dear Maddy."

She drew down the sheet, which shrouded the figure, as she spoke, and gazed at the dead body of her husband. His daughter also looked at it in silence.

"Poor papa," sighed Ethel, at last. "How much happier he would be at this moment, if he had only considered others a little, as well as himself."

"Mumsey," said Madeline, in an awed whisper, "Do you think he is in heaven?"

"O Maddy dear, don't ask me. I hope so; I do, indeed; for it is so terrible to think otherwise; but we are told that only those who love God can go to heaven, and, therefore, I do not know what to think. But we can always pray for him, my dear, that his sins may be forgiven, and that he may find hope and peace at the last."

"It seems so strange to me," replied the girl, as she gazed at the placid face of the dead; "he looks so calm, so much at rest. And yet, when one remembers…"

"That is just what we must not do, my dear," exclaimed Ethel; "we must *not* remember. We must do our utmost to forget, and trust that God may have forgotten also."

"O Mumsey, that is such self-deception. God does *not* forget. How can He? And if He were inclined to do so, the lives that have been made so wretched by my father's means, would cry out against him from the ground."

"Maddy, you must not say such things. They are wicked. It is unnatural to hear a child speak thus of her own father."

"Then, what was it to hear a father speak to his own child, as papa spoke to my darling brother Gilbert? Take me away, Mumsey. Perhaps you are right; but your ideas are too high for me. I am only very human, and I can't forget. I don't think I ever shall, either in this world or the world to come."

"O, it is all very dark and miserable," cried Ethel. "I am so glad Doctor Barnes telegraphed for my darling mother. She is the best friend I have ever had. You are right, dear Maddy. This is no place for us. I thought we ought to come, but I was wrong. We should have waited till our memories were less keen and bitter. I meant to have said a prayer by his side; but the very sight of him lying here, as impassive to our sufferings, and deaf to our entreaties, as he was on earth, has driven it out of my head. Let us go back to our own rooms, dear, and pray for ourselves, that the trials we have undergone may have a salutary effect on us, and make us more considerate of the feelings of our fellow creatures."

The two women left the room with their arms twined round each other's waists; but without one backward glance to where the husband and father lay beneath his shroud.

"I can't stand this much longer," thought the Professor. "Is there no way by which I can escape being tortured after this fashion?"

"Not yet," answered a voice near him.

He turned, and saw a majestic figure standing by his side. It was that of a man, with a mild, calm, but decided expression. His hair and beard betokened that he had reached the prime of manhood; but his eyes were filled with the fire of youth. He was clothed in a long, flowing, white garment, something like the toga of the ancient Romans, which clung about his person, without incommoding his movements, and fell to his feet in straight, classical folds.

"Who are you?" asked the Professor. "I have never seen you before."

"Because your spiritual eyes have not been opened to perceive me," replied the man. "But I have been with you since you were born into the earth sphere. I am your controlling spirit; what you would call your guardian angel."

"But what is your name?"

"You can call me by the name by which I was known whilst I lived in this world—John Forest. I was a chemist and a scientist, like yourself. It is from my influence that your own proclivities arose."

"Why have you not discovered yourself to me before?"

"I was there, always; but you could not perceive me. Your eyes have been too much fixed on yourself and your pursuits, to feel a spiritual influence. The spirituality in you has been neglected, until it has burned down like the last flicker of an expiring rush-light. It was time you left this sphere, for soon it would have been extinguished altogether."

"But, if you possess any power, I beg of you to take me from this place. I have done with earth, it seems. Why cannot I quit it, and go either to heaven—or hell?"

"Don't be in a hurry. You will go to the place you have made for yourself, soon enough. At present, my orders are to keep you here. You have much to learn, and to endure. The first of your lessons begins in this house."

"You will not leave me?" said the Professor, trembling.

"No; God never leaves any one of His creatures alone. I shall be near you, though you may not see me."

"But tell me, why must I stay by this horrible body? What link is there, now, between it and me?"

"You stay because you cannot free yourself. You have lived for that body alone; you have riveted the chain between it and your spirit, until it is so fast that it is impossible to break it all at once. Have patience, and it will be broken. But I do not promise you that your next experience will be pleasanter."

"Why must I listen to all the rubbish the friends I have left behind talk of me? Cannot you close my ears? It annoys me."

"I know it does, because you feel it to be true. That is the first lesson you are ordained to learn—the A B C of your spiritual progress. What you hear, you have dictated for yourself. It is the effect of your own conduct whilst on earth. Until you know what you have lost, and what you might have gained, there will be no progression for you."

"Why are you going?"

"Because the time has not arrived for me to instruct you. Whilst you remain here, learn for yourself."

Again, the Professor was left alone with the decaying thing which had been his earthly envelope; and all night he had to stand beside it, viewing the progress of its corruption, and noting, sadly, that it lay there alone, as he was. He had heard, in bygone times, of how disconsolate widows and orphans spent days and nights in agony, praying beside their dead, struggling with their despair, and fainting under the sense of their irrevocable loss. But no one came to weep or pray over him. The house was very hushed and silent. No sounds of laughter, or loud talking, reached him where he stood; but the Professor remembered that his home had never been a merry one. He had chidden his children whenever they happened to make an unwonted noise, because it interfered with his studies; and they had, generally, carried their mirth out of doors, or into the houses of other people. It was nothing very uncommon, therefore, to find the house silent. Late at night there came the undertaker's men to measure his corpse for its coffin. The Professor thought they did it in a very unfeeling manner. They did not laugh or talk much. They hurried over the proceedings in a most business-like way, one man taking his length and breadth, with a tape measure, whilst the other wrote the numbers down in a memorandum book; and James stood by with the utmost indifference.

"Going to have a first-class funeral, I hear," said one of the undertakers to the servant.

"O, yes; I've no doubt of it," he replied. "I s'pose the widder has got all the money, so it's the least she can do. They weren't over and above sweet on one another during his life-time, and they're allays the ones as tries to make it up with a big splash afterwards."

"She's a nice lady, though, and a pretty one, is your missus," said the other.

"Ah, she is that; and didn't get any too good a time of it, I can tell you, what with his fads and his tempers. Why, his only son, a nice young gentleman, too, ran away from home, yesterday afternoon; and Mary, the housemaid, she do say that she was on the upper landing while the row was a going on, and Master Gilbert, he up with his fist, and hit the master right in the eye."

"And sarve him right, too, if he ill-treated the lad," observed the undertaker's man. "I've got nine on 'em myself, and find it hard work, sometimes, to put bread in their mouths; but I've never hit one on 'em in their lives, and never will. Lor! go against one's own flesh and blood! I'd be afraid to face my Maker if I did. Come on, Bill. I've got it all down. The shell will be round the fust thing in the morning, mister, and the outer coffin by nightfall. I hear the funeral's to be on Thursday. Sharp work, eh?"

"Well, I don't s'pose she'll want to keep 'un here longer than necessary; and the sooner these jobs is over the better, to my mind. I daresay the pore missus will be wanting to get away for a holiday. She hasn't had one since I came into the house, and that I can swear."

The Professor was indignant at hearing this conversation; but he had no power of refuting the men's arguments; so he was compelled to listen in silence, whether he would or no, and was thankful when the business was concluded, and they left him in peace. Not quite in peace, however; for, though he was still human enough to feel angry and injured by the opinions he heard from all sides, he was already beginning to wonder if what they said was true. His brain was now his most powerful organ. The desires and weaknesses of the body had, in a measure, left him, though he still felt their influence; but his brain was in fuller working power than it had been whilst clothed with the flesh. He could think more clearly, see more clearly, and reflect more clearly than he had ever done in life; and his thoughts kept wandering back to his son, Gilbert, and the probable future that lay before him. Would the sins of it, and the miseries of it all lie at his door, as Ethel had told him, the night before? Would he be obliged to expiate the frailties or crimes which his undue harshness might cause his son to commit?

"Yes," replied the voice of John Forest, by his side; "even unto the third and fourth generation."

"My God, it will be hell," said the Professor.

"It *will* be hell," replied the voice.

The Professor's head sunk upon his breast. Already, in so short a time—only four and twenty hours after he had quitted his body—his eyes were beginning to see daylight, like the eyes of a blind-born puppy opening to the wonderment of life.

The following day the Professor had more visitors. His wife again stole into the room, accompanied by her mother, Mrs. Fellows. They looked at the corpse for a few minutes in complete silence; for, however bad or unpleasant a man may have been, death is a solemn matter for all of us; and the less hope we entertain of a fellow-creature's happiness in the other world, the more solemn it becomes. Ethel's face was very grave; so was that of her mother; but neither of them had been crying. The Professor could see that plainly.

"Death is a terrible thing, mother," said Mrs. Aldwyn, "especially when it comes so suddenly."

"I quite agree with you, my dear child," replied Mrs. Fellows; "but, at the same time, I cannot but perceive that this is a most blessed release for you. O my darling! how often, since your ill-fated marriage have I lain awake at night, praying to God to make some way of escape for you. You have been miserable. I know it well. You are not the same girl who was married in Beer church two years ago. You look ten years older. How can you expect me to be sorry for an event that opens out a happier future for you?"

"No, darling mother; I suppose not. But it was my own fault. I married him with my eyes open; so I have no right to complain."

"You married him because we were so poor, and you thought one mouth less to feed at home would be a relief to your father and me. Don't try to make the sacrifice less, my dearest girl. We recognized it, and thought it noble of you. But had I known he would have treated you as he has, curbing all your innocent enjoyments, and trying to transform your bright nature into a copy of his own, I would have seen you dead, sooner than you should have thrown yourself away on him."

"Never mind, dearest mother. It is all over now, thank God; and we must try and forget it. But I am almost frightened for poor Maddy. She is grieving so bitterly for her brother, that I cannot persuade her even to think kindly of her father. All she says is: 'Don't mention the subject to me, please. Let me try and forget he ever lived. If I don't, I shall say something to shock you.' Isn't it dreadful, mother, a daughter to feel so with regard to her own father?"

"It may be very dreadful, my dear; but the dreadful part of it lies with the father, and not with the daughter. A man who goes through life selfishly seeking his own comfort, and aims and ends, without the least regard to those of his wife and children, cannot expect to be mourned when he passes away. 'As ye have sown, so shall ye reap.'[12] It is the law of retribution."

"It is very, very sad," said Ethel, gazing at her husband's corpse.

"It would have been sadder still if he had lived, my child; so put away all false sentiment, and be thankful for your release. Don't stay in this room; it will only make you morbid."

The elder lady turned to leave, as she spoke; but the wife lingered a moment by the silent figure on the table.

"Goodby, Henry," she murmured, as she laid a little bouquet of roses in the dead man's hands. "We were very unhappy together; but, perhaps, I was in fault as much as you. Let us try to forgive each other; and, then, some day, we may meet again in peace. I wonder if you can see and hear me now, and read my heart, and know how sorry I am that our married life was such a disappointment for us both."

How hard the Professor tried to speak, and tell her that he was also sorry for the past. But his words of repentance were borne away, voiceless, on the air; and not the suspicion of a whisper reached the ears of his girl-wife.

"Mother," she said, presently, turning to Mrs. Fellows, "ought I to kiss him? They say if you don't touch a corpse you dream of it. Is it a duty? Ought I?"

"Take me away from this place, for Heaven's sake," exclaimed the Professor, faintly, "or it will kill me."

"These are idle words. Nothing could kill you whilst on earth; nothing can kill you now. You will live for ever and ever. How you live depends upon yourself. But, if you wish to leave your body now, you can. Come!"

The controlling spirit stretched forth his hand, and grasped that of the Professor. He experienced a sensation as though he were being pressed downwards against water; but, before he could express any surprise at the novelty of it, he found himself standing with John Forest on an illimitable plane of open country.

---

[12] This is not a direct quote from the Bible but the idea can be found in at least two places: Galatians chpt 6, v. 7 'Be not deceived; God is not mocked: for whatsoever a man soweth, that shall he also reap.' Job chpt 4, v. 8 'Even as I have seen, they that plow iniquity, and sow wickedness, reap the same.' The parable of the sower is found in Matthew chpt 13, v. 3-8.

"Certainly not, my dear, if you don't feel inclined. For my part, I shouldn't think of such a thing. He wasn't a kissable person during his life-time, and, I am sure, he isn't after his death."

"I couldn't! I couldn't!" returned her daughter with a shudder, as she turned and followed Mrs. Fellows from the room.

- CHAPTER FIVE -

THE PROFESSOR MEETS HIS FRIENDS

The Professor gazed around him with surprise. On the greensward, beneath his feet, were dotted innumerable flowers, such as he had known upon the lower earth—daisies, buttercups and dandelions. A river ran through the campaign; and, in the distance, he could perceive belts of trees, and fields of waving corn and barley.

"To what part of the habitable globe have you brought me, John Forest?" he asked. "This is not England, as far as I can see, and yet I seem to recognize the surroundings."

"If, by the habitable globe, you mean the insignificant planet we term the earth," replied his guide, "this country has nothing whatever to do with it. You are standing now in one of the first or lowest spheres. It is called the 'Sphere of Meeting'; for here, if you have any friends, eager to welcome you to the Spiritual World, you will have an opportunity of seeing and being recognized by them."

The Professor looked around him, eagerly. There was a large mass of men, women and children walking up and down the flower be-gemmed grass, every now and then turning their eyes towards the entrance of the long stretch of country, as fresh groups of spirits arrived, under the charge of their guardian angels.

The Professor witnessed more than one glad greeting in the first few seconds he stood there; and began to wonder when he should see his father and mother, and his first wife, Susan Clumber. He had not always been the cold-natured, selfish creature who had just left the earth body. There had been a time when, if he had yielded to the gentle counsel and entreaties of a woman who loved him, he might have turned out a very different man; but he had allowed his lower nature to get the better of his spiritual inclinations, and so she, Susie, his first wife, and the only woman who had ever excited anything like love in his breast, had faded out of life, weary of trying to incite him to a better and nobler existence, and he had hived onto insult her pure memory in the ears of her only son. The Professor had almost forgotten Susie whilst on earth; but, now that he witnessed several happy and excited greetings passing between reunited husbands and wives, his thoughts reverted to her, and he mentally pictured how pleasant it would be to find himself received into her open arms, and permitted to forget all the annoyances of earth, in the solace and renewal of his early love. He was looking eagerly into the faces of the women who passed up and down before him, for a glimpse of her, when John Forest asked him whom he was seeking.

"My wife, Susan Clumber," he answered, "tell me how I can find her. Is she living on this plane?"

"That I do not know," was the reply. "But, if there is a strong attraction between you, she is sure to know, by intuition, that you have arrived, and will hasten to meet you here."

"There is my father," exclaimed the Professor, excitedly, pointing with his finger; "there, do you not see that old man, with the long beard? That is my father, Doctor Benjamin Aldwyn. He was a well-known surgeon on earth. Let me go to him. He will give me all the information and assistance I require. And that is my brother George and my sister Mary walking with him. O, do let me go and make myself known to them."

"By all means," said John Forest, loosing his hand; "and when you have done so you can come back here and tell me of your success."

The Professor flew from his grasp, like an arrow from a bow, and joined the group he had pointed out. It consisted of the relations he had described; but it was to his father that the Professor addressed himself first.

"Father," he exclaimed, with outstretched hands; "you know me, do you not? I am your son, Henry. I have just come over from the earth plane, and I feel so lonely here. How glad I am to meet you!"

"Why?" demanded the old man, without advancing to greet his son.

"Because—" stammered the Professor; "but why should you

ask me? Why should I *not* be pleased to meet you and my brother and sister again?"

"The affections which we have neglected to cultivate whilst on earth are not born and ripened to perfection in a day, Henry," was the reply. "Where were you when I lay dying, and eagerly counting the moments of my life ebbing away, lest they should all go before I had given my forgiveness and blessing to my ungrateful son."

"I did not know— I never imagined—"

"No quibbles here," said the father, sternly. "There is no possibility of deception in these spheres. You declined to believe I was dying, because, in your selfishness, you were engaged on some experiments which had cost you money; and you feared it would be wasted, if interrupted. So your father left the world without bidding you farewell, unknowing that once quit of the burden of the flesh, his spiritual sight would be so clear that he would no longer have any desire to see or communicate with you."

"Is that possible?" cried the unhappy Professor. "Will you not recognize me, then, as your child—your son?"

"The ties of nature are not recognized here, unless they have been accompanied by the ties of the spirit. What sympathy do you expect my spirit to have with yours? I see you now as you are. A man eaten up with love of self, with less spirituality than many a little child; for you have trodden it under foot, and dwarfed and stunted it, until it has dwindled down to an abortion. Had you given the reins to the natural love God implanted in your breast, for the good of your fellow creatures, you would have nourished and enlarged it; but, as it is, you have nearly killed it. The only thing which survives the pettiness of earth, is Love. If you cannot bring that in your hand I see nothing to communicate with. There can be no fellowship between God and Belial."[13]

"Shall we never be anything to one another again, then?" asked the Professor. "I remember boxy proud you used to be of my success in science, and said I was destined to make the old name

---

[13] See II Corinthians chpt 6, v. 15 'And what agreement hath Christ with Belial? Or what part hath he that believeth with an infidel?' See also John Milton's 'Paradise Lost' Bk 1, 490.

famous. I have succeeded beyond my utmost hopes. My writings are a power in Europe; my experiments followed with the keenest interest, and my decisions listened to with interest and attention. What do you want more? Have I not fulfilled the highest hopes you ever entertained for me?"

"Your experiments—your success—your decisions," repeated the old man, with contempt; "what value are they, do you suppose, to us in the blessed freedom of spirituality? Less than the dirt beneath your feet. The humblest, most ignorant creature on earth, who passes over here with a heart overflowing with love for his kind, is placed on a higher eminence than a king or a philosopher, who has lived only for himself and his own success. Look at the spirit who enters the sphere at the present moment."

The Professor glanced in the direction indicated by his father's gesture, and saw a poor, crippled form being supported into the sphere. Her features were seamed and scarred as by some terrible disease; her figure was bent nearly double; her eyes were swollen as with many tears, and her face weary and careworn. She looked round her fearfully, but expectantly, as she appeared amongst them. But a shriek of joy heralded her approach. From every part of the plane came flying happy, joyous spirits, who crowded round the poor, fainting figure, and embraced and blessed her, and bore her away amongst them, when, to his astonishment, the Professor saw that she was suddenly transformed. Her lameness and scars had disappeared, and her features wore a hook of spiritual beauty that transformed them to an angelic radiance.

"What is the meaning of it?" he asked his father.

"The meaning is self-obvious. This woman, poor, diseased and ungainly, had yet a heart so full of love that she forgot her own sufferings in trying to alleviate those of her fellow-creatures. So her reward has come. Freed from the shackles of earth, she enters upon eternal happiness. She could not miss it. The Master had promised it to her: 'Inasmuch as ye have done it unto one of the least of these, my brethren, ye have done it unto Me.'"[14]

---

[14] Matthew chpt 25, v. 40 'And the King shall answer and say unto them, Verily I say unto you, Inasmuch as ye have done it unto one of the least of these my

The Professor turned to regard his own features in a running brook close by. They were not in the least altered. He still possessed the sandy hair and mottled complexion, on which the layers-out had commented so uncomplimentally.

"But what has changed her so?" he asked; "I am not changed."

"It is love that has changed her—the love of God—and happiness that glorifies her countenance," replied the old man. "Do you think that spirits carry their diseases and deformities into the spiritual world? That would be impossible. Even when we pass away at an advanced age, as I did, we renew our youth as soon as the spirit within us commences to soar upwards. When the body entirely leaves us, with all its associations, memories and regrets, we shine as the stars in heaven; but not till then."

"But you look the same to me, father. I recognized you directly. You are not changed!"

"In reality, I am; but your eyes are still carnal; so you see me as they depict me—as rose-coloured glasses make all things rose-colour. When you have learned to recognize the love of God, my son, as seen through the love of your fellow-men, you, too, will be changed."

"And till then—" said the Professor, mournfully.

"Till then I have not the power, if I had the will, to remain near you. In this world we cannot force ourselves to be outwardly affectionate, when, inwardly, we feel estranged. There is no deception here. All thoughts are revealed; and the very difference in our spirits must necessarily keep us apart. You must have perceived that neither your brother nor sister have appeared to recognize your presence. It is because they do not see you. They passed away when still young, and have not preserved their carnal proclivities as forcibly as I have. Their spirits are not in touch with yours. They have not even heard our conversation."

"Then, am I to be banished from the company of my own family forever?" exclaimed the Professor in despair.

"Not so. When you have purified yourself through the exercise of love, we shall be able to communicate more freely. Farewell!"

---

brethren, ye have done it unto me.'

"Stay, father, one moment, for pity's sake. Tell me where I can find Susan, my first wife. She, at least, will not quite have forgotten our early love."

"Have you not perceived her presence? She is walking just in front of you, between those two little children—the still-born babies, over the loss of which she so much grieved."

"That girl beside the weeping willow tree? But she looks quite young, not more than twenty. And Susie was thirty-five when she died."

"Nevertheless, that is she. She was a loving, single-hearted woman. There was no obstacle to her progressing as soon as she came over to our side."

"But those children—they cannot be mine. I have only Madeline and Gilbert, who are both alive. These were born dead; how can they live here?"

"They assuredly owe their earthly bodies to you. In the earthly sense, you are their father, though I do not think you will be allowed to communicate with them at present. But there is no death for those into whom God has breathed the breath of life. They lived before they were born; therefore, they live forever. And that girl, as you call her, leading them by the hand, is Susan, their mother."

"I must speak to her. Surely, surely, she cannot bear resentment, so kind and gentle as she was. She will receive me as if she were still on earth, and give me protection and shelter."

The Professor followed in the wake of Susan as he spoke. She had been a pretty woman whilst on earth, but she was much prettier now. Her fair hair hung down her neck in waving ringlets; her large blue eyes were soft and ambient; her graceful figure was draped with consummate taste, and her head and waist were wreathed with flowers. In either hand she held a child—one, a little boy, with dark locks and a brown, ruddy countenance; the other, a girl, as fair and gentle-looking as herself. As the Professor remembered these charming children were his own, his spirit glowed with expectation; and he thought it impossible that their mother could accord him as uncongenial a reception as his father had done. He advanced towards her, softly, lest she should be startled, calling her by her name of "Susan! Susan!" She turned and looked at him.

"Who are you," she inquired, "who calls me by my earthly name?"

"Who am I? Cannot you see? Your husband, Henry Aldwyn."

Susan regarded him attentively, but gravely.

"Now, that I look at you closely, I see that you are," she replied, but without any further greeting. "How long have you been here?"

"Have you no better welcome for me than that?" he asked, in a tone of disappointment.

"I am glad, for your own sake, that you are freed from the fetters of the flesh; but I fear there must be a bitter penance in store for you."

"But are you not glad to see me again, Susan? It is ten years since we parted. Do you remember your last illness, and how I took you to Hastings to try if the sea air would revive you, and how hard I tried to atone for any little disagreeableness that may have occurred before it."

"Yes, because I was dying," she replied; "but, had I recovered, it would have been the same thing over again. You never really cared for any one but yourself, Henry, and, I fear, the habit is not purged out of you, even yet."

"Then you have quite forgotten our early love—the days of our honeymoon—the time when you thought me all that a man should be?"

"O, no; but I cannot remember them without remembering, also, how bitterly I was deceived. We should never have come together, Henry. We are too opposite in character to assimilate either in that world or this."

"Do you repudiate me, the same as my father and brothers and sisters have done?" he demanded, bitterly.

"No; there is no question of repudiation; but here there is no dissembling. I cannot tell you how much I had to dissemble whilst I lived with you on earth, in order to preserve peace in the house. My life was a life of deception. People called me amiable; but I was simply a deceiver. God mercifully delivers us from that here. If our spirits are not in sympathy with another spirit, we cannot stay near him. Something in our magnetism drives us as wide asunder as the two poles of the earth. It is not our doing; it is God's decree. The only attraction here is when two spirits are in perfect sympathy with one another."

"And, doubtless, you have already found another spirit to sympathize with yours?" remarked the Professor, ironically. But Susan took his words in perfect good faith.

"Yes," she answered, simply; "I was mated soon after I passed over. My affinity is no one whom I ever knew on earth. He lived many hundreds of years before I was born. But, of a necessity, he makes me happy. One cannot be unhappy in the sphere to which, by God's goodness, I have attained."

"If you do not live on this sphere, why did you come here this morning?" asked the Professor.

"I was told to come," replied Susan. "We are all under the orders of Almighty God. Perhaps it was to meet you. I did not ask, and I do not know. Our only duty is to obey."

The Professor was still so human that his feelings were becoming very much ruffled by her calm demeanour. He had always expected, in a vague way, that, when he met his first wife again, all the differences of their married life would be dissolved, in some miraculous manner, and they would be lovers again for eternity. But all was so different from what he had been led to believe.

"At all events," he said, rather roughly, "these children are mine, and, I suppose, I have the right to ask to look at them."

Susan regarded him with calm surprise.

"These children!" she echoed. "O, no; how should they be? All of them that belonged to you lies in Kensal Green Cemetery.[15] Their spirits, happily for them, never lived to know you. They are essentially God's little ones—too pure for contact with any one so fresh from earth as you are. They do not understand your language. They could not communicate with you if they would, or if I would

---

[15] The General Cemetery of All Souls, Kensal Green was established by the General Cemetery Company. Designed by John Griffith, the greater part of it was consecrated by the Bishop of London on 24 January 1833. The first person to be entombed in the cemetery was Margaret Gregory on 31 January 1833. Marryat was buried here after her death in 1899.

permit them," she added slowly.

"You are complimentary," said the Professor.

"Don't tempt me to be more so, Henry," she replied. "Why should I wish these pure, little spirits to communicate with your gross one? What else but harm could you do them? What have you done with the children God entrusted to your care? Where is my Gilbert? What is my Madeline growing up like?"

"They have elected to go their own way," he answered, sullenly, "and must take the consequences. They have been stubborn and unruly from the beginning. And, now I am freed from the control of them, they will have to shift for themselves."

"So much the worse would it be for you if it were so, Henry. But you mistake. Your purification will have to be worked out through these very children. The purgatory[16] before you will be increased, or lessened, as you undo the wrong you have wrought them in the past. They were a solemn charge committed to your keeping, and you have woefully neglected it. Do you think God means to lose these two souls, or to condemn them to punishment, whilst *you*, the author of their rebellion, are able to suffer in their stead? This is why you have been called away from earth so early and so suddenly. I see it now. The future of Madeline and Gilbert lie, in a great measure, in your hands. By working out their salvation you will secure your own. There will be no place for you here, till that task is accomplished."

"Do you mean that I am to have no rest, then? That, after fifty-five years of toil, I have been called away, only to be set a harder task than I have ever had yet—the reclamation of these two unloving and rebellious children?"

"Unloving, because you have never loved them; rebellious, because you have set them an example of rebellion against your Maker. Yes; I mean what I said. Your future work does not lie here, but *there*," said Susan, as she pointed downward towards the earth.

"No one wants me here, and no one wants me there," exclaim-

---

[16] The teaching of the Catholic church (to which Marryat converted) states that purgatory is a purification process which a sinner has to go through in order to enter heaven and the presence of God.

ed the unhappy Professor. "Where shall I find rest for the sole of my feet? This is hell, indeed."

"It is," replied Susan, gently; "the hell you have made for yourself. There is no heaven and no hell in reality, Henry—not such as we are wrongly taught from infancy to believe in. We make our heaven, or we make our hell. What greater hell could there be than for a man to find (as you have just said) that no one wants him here, and no one wants him there? That the inhabitants of earth are glad to get rid of him, and the denizens of the spheres have forgotten that he existed? And the reason is, because nothing but love lives forever. You have not cultivated that love in those around you; what, then, have they to miss when you leave them? What treasure have you laid up for yourself in heaven to draw upon at this eventful crisis of your life? I loved you whilst on earth. You made me unhappy; still I loved you; for women are weak, and must have something to cling to whilst in the body; and I was always hoping that, some day, you might return my love. But you know that you never did. I lived and died a disappointed woman; but, as soon as I came over here, I grieved no more, because, with my spiritual eyes, I could see you were not worth grieving for. If you picked up what you believed to be a diamond of value, in the street, you would preserve it with the utmost care; but, if a jeweller proved to you that it was only glass, you would throw it back into the nearest gutter. Spirituality is the great jeweller who tests our diamonds for us, Henry, and when we perceive their worthlessness we cease to lament their loss."

"O, God!" moaned the miserable man. "Thou art teaching me by means of a bitter lesson, indeed."

"But not one that will last forever, Henry," said Susan; "and the sooner it begins, the sooner will it be accomplished."

"How am I to begin it?"

"Ask your spirit guide to take you back to earth, and help you to remedy the evils you have wrought. You have left an unjust will behind you: unjust and ungenerous to the poor, young creature who took my place, and whom you have made almost as unhappy as you made me. You have driven our son, Gilbert, from your doors, and incited him to an act of folly, for which he will have to pay bitterly; and you have, by your inconsideration and harshness, turned Madeline's heart against you, till she is ready to curse your very memory. Are these not things calling for God's vengeance, unless you try to remedy them?"

"How is it possible? Who will teach me how to do so? How can I, being out of my body, influence those who yet remain on the earth?"

"Had you cultivated your spirit more whilst you lived there, you would not have to ask me such a question," replied Susan. "You would know that half the deeds, either for good or evil, committed by mortals, are instigated by the influence of spirits. But your guide can teach you that better than myself. Farewell."

"And you can part with me thus, Susan! My wife! The only woman I ever loved!" he cried, in the agony of his remorse.

She turned, and regarded him compassionately.

"You have never met *your* wife yet, Henry; but you will, some day, and be as happy as you will make her. But you must be purified first, as though by fire."

As she disappeared beneath the grove of trees, holding her infants by the hand, the Professor turned to seek John Forest.

"Take me away from here," he exclaimed, bitterly; "I am neither known, nor wanted. I am friendless, homeless, and alone."

"As you have made Gilbert," said his guide.

"Don't torture me more than is necessary, for God's sake. The bitterness of hell is on me now. If you have the power, take me hence."

As the Professor spoke the words, he found himself back in the familiar precincts of his own house.

- CHAPTER SIX -

HOME AGAIN

As the Professor passed the library door, he gave an involuntary shudder.

"Is that—that—*thing* there still?" he asked.

John Forest smiled.

"Certainly not. It was buried three months ago. You left your earthly body in March. It is now June. Cannot you see that the trees are in leaf, and the birds are singing?"

"But how can that be?" asked the Professor, in a bewildered tone. "I was only a few hours, surely, in the spiritual sphere."

"You may have thought so; but you mistake. We have no time in eternity. You were longer passing from one world to the other than you imagined. Your spirit needed rest after so sudden a transit, and I gave it you. Now, you are in your old home again, and better able to judge of the effects your management has left behind it."

"Where shall I go first?" asked the Professor, trembling.

"Why not visit your wife? You will find her in the drawing-room. Surely you have not forgotten the way?"

"No; but it seems so strange, so extraordinary, to find myself here. All my links to this world are dissolved. I have no interest left in it."

"Have you any stronger ties in the other? Wherever you go, you will find it the same. Your heart is shrivelling up within itself from want of exercise. Let it expand, and the cords of love, which will shoot from it, will tie you, all too firmly, to both the worlds, in which you now find no companionship."

As he said these words, John Forest disappeared; and the Professor glided into the drawing-room, alone.

It was filled with the scent of flowers. Bowls, full of roses and lilies and mignonette, adorned the tables, whilst in the window recesses stood jardinieres of growing plants, which filled the air with their fragrance. The Professor's first feeling was one of indignation that Ethel should have wasted so much money. How often he had refused to let her purchase a few flowers, though he knew how dearly she loved them, and that, down at her own home in Devonshire, she had been used to enjoy them in profusion all the year round. But, then, he remembered he had lost the power to find fault with her simple, innocent tastes. She had the handling of the money now; it was too late for him to think of objecting to what she did with it. Yet, it went to his soul to smell those flowers, blooming in a London drawing-room in June. He wondered, too, if she had ever placed so much as a rose upon his tomb in Kensal Green Cemetery, where, he concluded, they had buried his body in the family vault.

The next object his eyes took in was the form of Ethel, herself. How very much younger and prettier and happier she looked than she had done whilst he was on earth. She was dressed in deep black, certainly; but it was not his idea of a widow's attire.[17] She wore no cap upon her head, and her gown was not trimmed with crape. Her soft, abundant, brown hair was piled just in the old fashion, on the top of her head; and, in her bosom, she wore a bunch of violets—actually, violets. The Professor thought her dress was quite indecent, considering he had only been gone for three months. Besides, what was she doing in town in the height of the season?[18] It would certainly have been more decorous for a recently-afflicted widow to hide her grief down at Worthing, or Bognor, or some equally dull watering-place. As he was musing

---

[17] A widow was expected to be in deep mourning for a year and a day after the death of her husband, wearing deep black with absolutely no trim and in England a widow's cap was expected. Deep mourning was followed by a further 18 months during which mourning attire was gradually lessened.
[18] There was a general code of behaviour which widows were expected to follow. It was generally the custom that a widow should not leave the house for the first month after the death of her husband except to go to church. After the first month she could go out and receive callers but nothing of a frivolous nature could be undertaken. After three months she could attend limited social events but should still be wearing deep mourning. Only after deep mourning had finished could she re-enter society. However it was considered unseemly for a widow to receive gentlemen-callers for at least another 18 months.

thus, James entered the room. James used to be attired in a plain, black suit, like a doctor's servant; now he flamed forth in livery—drab coat, with silver buttons and dark-green plush breeches—very handsome, no doubt; but decidedly not mourning. What could it all mean? The poor Professor fumed and fussed, as he stood by the window curtains, and noted these signs of forgetfulness of his wishes and commands.

"Captain Standish, if you please, ma'am," said James.

"O, show him up at once," exclaimed Ethel, joyfully.

The Professor ground his teeth. How joyously she spoke. What a happy ring of freedom there was in her voice. And all for that Captain Standish, that *dear* cousin Ned; the man he had said, almost with his last breath, she should never see again. It was abominable. It was too bad. There was no gratitude or affection in the world. And this was the girl he had raised from poverty to a condition of affluence. If it could only have been kept from him; but to have to see and listen to it all. This was, indeed, retribution.

Cousin Ned entered the room with a familiar and jaunty air; an air of being certain of his welcome. It was, evidently, not the first time he had seen the widow since she had become such.

"Well, my dear Ethel, and how are you this morning? Jolly?" he commenced. "Hadn't we a pleasant time last evening? I don't know when I have enjoyed a concert so much. I am so glad I persuaded you to go."

"You could not have enjoyed it more than I did," replied Ethel, smiling; "only I was afraid people would say it was rather soon for me to be seen in public."

"Hang people," was the hearty rejoinder. "What does it signify what they say, or think? It is ridiculous to suppose a young creature like you is to shut herself up *ad infinitum*. It isn't as if you had ever cared for the man, nor as if he had made you a good husband. But you have been miserable quite long enough, in my opinion, and I shall get you out as often as I can whilst I am on shore."

"You're awfully kind to me, dear Ned," replied Ethel, with a blush.

"*Kind!*" repeated the Professor to himself, with a premonition of what was coming.

"No news of Gilbert, yet?" demanded the Captain.

Ethel's face changed.

"No," she said, shaking her head; "and I am beginning to be so nervous about him. Mr. Tredwell, my solicitor, says he cannot have shipped to sea under his own name, as he has searched all the books, and there is not a Gilbert Aldwyn amongst them. And yet, he says, if the lad had not gone to sea, the police would have been sure to have traced him on shore."

"I think, so far, he is right," replied Captain Standish. "You see, there are always dozens of ships lying in the docks, which find themselves, at the last moment, short of hands; and, if Gilbert found his way down there, it is nine chances to one that he got employment the same day, and sailed the following morning. Else, I can't account for his not having heard of, or seen the announcement of his father's death. He would surely have returned home to you in that case."

"O, yes," said Mrs. Aldwyn; "Gilbert was very fond of me, but he had rather an obstinate disposition—"

"Like his charming father—" interposed cousin Ned.

"Well, what can you expect, Ned?" said his hostess, apologetically. "It is not the poor children's fault if they inherit it from him. Maddy is just the same; indeed, a great deal worse. She has given me a lot of trouble since her father's death; not that she is not just as affectionate as ever; but she is determined to go her own way, and will not listen to my advice. The fact is, the Professor curbed both Gilbert and Madeline so unnaturally tight, that, now they have got their heads, you must expect them to bolt. But, to return to Gilbert; his last words were that he would never come back whilst 'that man' (meaning his father) lived. So I think, with you, that, had he heard of his death, he would have returned immediately."

"If he has shipped, then, as a cabin boy, or cook, or the Lord knows what," continued the Captain, "we must conclude that he did go under an assumed name, which makes it very difficult to trace him. However, these trading voyages seldom last more than a few months; so we may confidently hope to see him back before long. He will make some inquiries about home, as soon as he touches shore again; and then he will hear the good news, and come back to his little Mumsey."

"O, I hope so; I sincerely hope so," said Ethel. "I am longing to make up to the dear boy for the harsh treatment he received. Ned, I do feel so thankful I did not bring a child into the world. Fancy having a son or daughter with that man's disposition. It would have broken my heart. It is quite bad enough to have to battle with it in my step-children."

"Is Maddy giving you so much trouble, then, Ethel?"

"The trouble is more on her own account than mine. She will not give up the acquaintanceship of the Reynolds; and I am more than afraid that she has a sort of a fancy for the oldest son, Wilfred, the young photographer, you know."

"Not that dreadful young cad? Surely, Maddy has better taste than that. Why, his manners are too offensive, even, for his trade. I never felt more like kicking a man than when I accompanied you to his studio."

"Ned, we women are such blind fools where our hearts are concerned, that we neither see nor hear, nor believe anything, or anybody, but the person for whom we have conceived a fancy. That is one reason that I long so much for Gilbert's return. I think he might influence his sister; for she is very much attached to him. She listens to me, but she does not heed what I say. If I point out to her (which I have done unscrupulously) that Mr. Reynolds is not in the same social position as herself, she only says: 'O, Mumsey, don't talk to me of birth and all that rubbish. I had enough of it with papa. What good did his birth do him, unless it was to make him more disagreeable than he was by nature. I've had enough of so-called gentlemen. Let me try one of the lower order, as a change. And I am very much afraid that she will—that it will end in a marriage. Of course, the Reynolds do all in their power to further it. Madeline, let alone the fact that she inherits money under the Professor's will, and may possibly have more, is a better match than they had any right to expect for their son; and they would be fools not to encourage the intimacy. But it will be a deplorable thing for her."

"Why do you say that Madeline is likely to have more money, Ethel? Where is it to come from?"

"Have you not heard the conditions of the Professor's will?" she asked him, with a deep blush.

"No! He left you comfortably off, I hope."

"O, yes; that is as long as I remain a widow," replied Ethel, blushing still more deeply.

"*Never?*" exclaimed Captain Standish, starting. "You don't mean to tell me he was so mean as that. That you are to lose your income if you marry again?"

"Yes, that is it. I have two thousand a year as long as I remain as I am at present; but, if I should elect to marry again, every penny of it goes to the children, unconditionally. So you see, the Professor never thought, apparently, that his daughter might wish to make an unsuitable marriage; yet, had he been asked, whilst on earth, to consent to her engagement to young Reynolds, he would have raved like a madman."

"Was Gilbert not mentioned in the will?"

"O, yes. He went so suddenly, you see, that, luckily, he had no time to alter it. The children share alike. Their portion gives them each about a couple of hundred a year; and mine goes to them, in equal parts, at my death or marriage. So they will be very comfortably off—that is, if I should marry again."

"And shall you, Ethel?" asked cousin Ned, in rather tender tones, as he took her hand. "Have you any proclivities that way, my dear; or has that man's treatment too utterly disgusted you with the holy state?"

"I don't know," replied Ethel, looking down. "No one has asked me yet. It will be time to decide when some one does."

"Listen to me, my darling. You know that, years ago, I loved you. You chose to quarrel with me because you got it into your foolish, little head that I had flirted with Maggie Robinson; but it was all a silly mistake, believe me. However, we quarrelled and parted; but all through that sad voyage I was thinking and hoping that, as soon as I reached land again, I should see you and convince you that I had never been untrue; and that the love-making to Miss Robinson existed in your brain alone. Well, after two years' absence, I came back, to find you married to Professor Aldwyn. What I felt, I had no right to tell you then; but I was nearly heart-broken. I went to sea again without seeing you, and we did not meet until last March. But all the time I was loving and longing for you, and you only; and now that you are free, I cannot help telling you so. Is there any hope for me, Ethel? Can you feel for your old sweetheart, as you once did, when we walked through the lanes of Beer together, and promised to wait for each other, to our lives' end? I think you loved me then. Do you love me now?"

The Professor expected to hear his widow make some remonstrance at her cousin addressing such words to her so soon after his lamented demise; but he was woefully mistaken. What Ethel did, was to creep closer to her objectionable cousin Ned, till she had reached the sanctuary of his waistcoat, when she burrowed her head in there, and whispered, in a very small voice:

"O Ned, it has been just the same with me. I have been miserable ever since we parted that wretched night in Green Man's lane. My heart seemed broken, too; so much so, that when the Professor proposed to me, and mother said it was a very good match, and father would be glad to get even one of us off his hands, I said 'Yes,' because I was really too hopeless to care what became of me. You didn't think I married him for love, Ned, surely. I never felt the least spark of it for him. He was kind at first, and I thought he would be my friend through life; but that dream soon vanished."

"My poor darling," cried cousin Ned, sympathetically; "you have suffered, indeed."

"Yes, but it is all over now," exclaimed Ethel, joyfully, as she raised her beaming face; "and you mustn't call me your 'poor' darling, ever again, Ned, for I am the very happiest woman in all the world."

"But hold hard," replied Captain Standish. "Don't be in such a hurry. What about the two thousand a year? It will vanish like a heavenly dream, if you have the bad taste to marry me."

"Like a bad dream, you mean, Ned; like a horrible nightmare that chained me to misery. Let the money go. Let Maddy and Gillie have it and everything else, so long as I have *you*."

"But I can't make so much as that, my Ethel," said Captain Standish, somewhat ruefully; "at least, I am afraid, not for some years to come. All I can offer you, dear love, is a cosy berth aboard my ship, and lots of love when we are together, to make up for the occasional absences which I must spend on deck."

"And will you really take me to sea with you, Ned!" cried Ethel, delightedly. "O, that will be charming! I do so love the sea, and everything connected with it; and I shall look upon the dear 'Devonshire' as my home. And then, to be always with you! O, it is too much," said the girl, crying with excitement.

"And you are sure you will have no regrets?" inquired the Captain, a little anxiously.

"Regrets for what? The money? O, you don't know me; you don't, indeed. I shall be glad to get rid of it. I want to owe nothing to anybody but you. If you knew what my life with him was; how I loathed it and him, and everything connected with my unhappy marriage, you would not ask me if I shall regret losing all memory of that wretched time, even at the expense of a few pounds, more or less. Ned, darling, do believe me, as you did when we strolled in the Devonshire lanes together: I love you, and you only; and I want nothing that you cannot give me, and no one who is not *you*."

"I do believe you, my dearest," said Captain Standish, as he kissed her passionately. "And I will take you at your word. How soon shall we be able to be married?"

"O, I'm afraid not for a long time," replied Ethel, with crimson cheeks. "You see, it is only three months yet, and, I suppose, the very least we can wait is a year."[19]

"Rubbish! Fiddlesticks!" cried cousin Ned. "Why, I've been waiting for you for four years already. What does a stupid conventionality signify to two longing hearts like ours? What difference can it make to a dead man, lying in his grave, whether his widow remains so for a month or a year? What do you owe to this man that you should consult the proprieties on his account? Who would be the wiser if I married you to-morrow, and carried you off

---

[19] See previous note – To marry so quickly would clearly be in defiance of all acceptable social codes.

in the 'Devonshire' next week?"

"O what a very unimportant person you must think me, to be able to leave my household in that indecorous manner. No, dear, we must not be quite so unconventional as all that. I would like it, Ned, oh, so dearly," said Ethel, with a sentimental sigh; "but I have my people at home and the children to consider, and a heap of things beside. So you must be a good boy, and rest content with being engaged to me for a few months longer."

"Well, well, I won't be greedy," replied the Captain. "I know that you are right. This unexpected happiness, however, is more than I deserve. What sweet dreams I shall have of home and you, when I am away. And next time I come back, perhaps…"

"Yes, next time, perhaps," echoed Ethel, with a beaming smile, as she softly laid her cheek on his; "we shall see what we shall see. O, how silly I am. You have made me wild with happiness, Ned. I hardly know what I am doing or saying. All the dark clouds of my life seem to have flown away forever."

"You have had your share of them, my darling," replied her cousin; "but, please God, the worst is over. My poor little Ethel in the clutches of that ogre! How I pitied you, though I dared not say so, when I called on you last March."

"And how very rude he was to you. I shall never forget it," said Ethel. "And if you could have seen him, after those two old men were gone, throwing all the lovely things you had brought me out of window, and kicking in the panels of my beautiful little cabinet, as if he would have liked to kick me. How I cried at the loss of them. What a brute I thought him. And then the next thing I heard was that he was dead. I tried to be sorry, Ned, but I couldn't. I only felt as if I had been chained fast in a prison and some one had come, as the angel did to Saint Peter, and knocked off my chains and set me free."[20]

"Free to love me for the rest of your life. Thank God for it!" exclaimed cousin Ned. "Never mind about the presents, my darling. No one shall ever dare to treat you so again, whilst I live to

---

[20] See The Acts of the Apostles, chpt 12, v. 1 – 11. St Peter, after being imprisoned by Herod, is helped to escape by the angel of the Lord.

defend you. The next voyage I make, we'll go to Japan together, and you shall buy everything you like best in the island, yourself. Won't that be better than my bringing them home to you?"

"O, lovely, exquisite!" acquiesced Ethel; and she repeated what she had said before: "Ned, dearest, darling Ned! I am the very happiest girl in all the world."

And the Professor had to stand by and hear and see it all.

- CHAPTER SEVEN –

A FACE IN THE CAMERA

"My time is up," said Captain Standish next, "and I must go. But I shall come again this evening, if you will let me, Ethel."

"If I will let you," repeated the girl after him, softly.

"And I will bring you a ring to wear on this dear, little hand," he added, raising it to his lips; "a ring that shall remind you of your true love far away, and that you have pledged yourself to him forever."

"O, no, dear Ned, not a ring," she answered; "he gave me one when we were engaged, and I used to hate it so. The signet of my bondage. Bring me a little, plain gold locket, with a piece of your bonny hair inside—a locket that I can wear next my heart, night and day, till we meet again. Nothing belonging to the Professor has ever lain near *that* yet," added Ethel, with a low laugh.

"How ungrateful women are," remarked the Professor to his guide; "I spent half I was worth on that girl when I first knew her, and hear how she speaks of my generosity."

"Had you spoken a few kind words to her afterwards," replied John Forest; "had you once or twice relinquished your own wishes in favour of hers, she would have treasured your gifts for the sake of it. But, money is valueless without love to sanctify it. She will value the least hair on Edward Standish's head, more than she did all your money or yourself."

"So it seems," said the Professor, bitterly.

He watched the lovers part with a fond embrace, and many promises of a speedy reunion.

"I am so happy—so happy," murmured Ethel, with feverish excitement, as she accompanied him to the door.

"And so am I, beloved," were his last words, as he passed through it.

But as soon as Captain Standish had gone, Mrs. Aldwyn's mood seemed to change. She became grave and thoughtful, and sat with her hands folded on her lap, gazing into space.

"What have I done," she thought (and though her lips uttered no words, the Professor found, to his surprise, that he could read all her thoughts, as though they had been spoken aloud), "to be so blest, I have never been a religious woman, though brought up so. Something in religion, as presented to me, jarred on my feelings; I have tried to do what appeared to be my duty, but it was done very grudgingly, and I feel myself to be a very unworthy individual, after all. And yet, God has sent me this exceeding happiness. How grateful to him I should be."

At that moment, the Professor perceived, to his amazement, the form of his first wife, Susan Clumber, standing behind Ethel. She looked just as she did when he met her in the spheres, but the children were not with her—she was alone. She was looking down upon Ethel with great tenderness, and as she stole her arm around her neck, the girl lifted her eyes to heaven (or where she had been told that heaven lay) and said, aloud:

"O God, I thank thee. Make me *more* thankful. Let all my future life resolve itself into a psalm of praise for Thine unexpected goodness to me."

"Is it possible," exclaimed the Professor, "that that is my wife, Susan? Why has she come down to the earth sphere? She never did so in my life-time."

"You speak in ignorance," replied John Forest. She has never ceased to visit her children, since she was called away from them. But what eyes had you to see her? What ears to hear her gentle counsels? Every good influence which has been brought to bear upon you—every whisper from your better self—every doubt whether, after all, you were quite just and right—has been prompted by the invisible presence of Susan. She has watched like a sister over your second wife; without her aid and solace, Ethel would hardly have been able to bear the trials you put upon her."

"They are two very handsome women," continued the Professor, as he saw the fair locks of Susan mingling with the darker tresses of Ethel. "I wonder it did not strike me so before. I knew they were nice-looking, but now they seem beautiful to me. Why is it?"

"Because, for the first time, you find yourself in a condition to perceive the beauties of their souls. Whilst you were on earth, you were so engrossed with your studies, and your own selfish designs, that you had no time to appreciate the minds of your life companions. They are both affectionate and kindly-natured women—you repressed their affection, and cruelly disregarded their feelings in every way. Consequently you alienated them from you, and you have lost them both."

"Will they never be mine again?"

"Never! through all eternity," replied his guide "and you would not be happy with them, if they were. They see your character too plainly. They despise it and you. What chance of happiness would there be for any of you?"

"Am I condemned then to pass through eternity alone?" groaned the Professor.

"Until you have remedied the evils you have wrought, by supplanting them with good. That is the Almighty decree. 'He shall not go thence until he have paid the uttermost farthing.'"[21]

"How can one undo what is done?"

"By doing it over again. When your son was a child, under your tuition, if he had brought you a sum, carelessly worked out, or a problem in Euclid[22] unproved, what should you have said to him?"

"Do it over again."

"Exactly so; and that is what the Almighty Spirit is saying to you at this moment. Rub out your faulty life and do it all over again. Rub out the evil—and fill in the void with deeds of righteousness and repentance."

"I do repent," said the Professor, "bitterly."

"That is the first stage, but only the first. You will find, now you have left your body, that something more is required than the idle words, 'I repent and I believe,' to secure your salvation. You

---

[21] Matthew chpt 5, v. 26 'Verily I say unto thee, Thou shalt by no means come out thence, til thou has paid the uttermost farthing.'
[22] Greek mathematician, (325BC – 265BC approx). Most famous of his publications was his treatise *The Elements*.

must work it out for yourself, in fear and trembling. God will not accept a sacrifice of empty words. You must bring fruits in your hands to lay upon his altar."

"I see plainly the miseries I have wrought by my behaviour in the earth life," said the Professor.

"O no, you don't. You deceive yourself," replied John Forest. "As yet you have only seen the good effected by your death. You have still to learn the evil which your selfish life caused, and which may extend from generation to generation. Here comes some of the fruit of it, in the person of your daughter Madeline. Mark her manner and her appearance.

At this juncture the door opened, rather noisily, and Madeline Aldwyn entered. Even the few months that had elapsed since her father's death seemed to have made a great change in her. She had always been a high-spirited girl, with something of the Professor's obstinacy and selfishness in her disposition, but these vices had been kept under by his severity to her. She had been afraid of him and the quarrels his displeasure engendered, the while she had hated and despised him for the very traits she had inherited. But, now that he had left her free and independent, her manners had vastly changed. She was still affectionate to her stepmother, but she would neither take her advice nor brook her interference. She came into the drawing-room now, a fine, handsome girl, dressed in black, of course, but with no appearance of mourning in her features. As she entered, Susan drew a little further away from Ethel's side, though she continued to stand by the two young women and listen to their conversation.

"Why does my former wife, who is the mother of Madeline, draw away from her own child, though she clings to a stranger like Ethel?" inquired the Professor.

"Because, though she loves Madeline, as being part of herself, the taint which you have left upon her is so strong as to prevent her mother getting as near to her as she can to Ethel, who has no blood of yours in her veins."

"That seems very hard," said the Professor.

"It may appear so to you, but it is the natural effect of a misused existence. In this world, spirits can converse with each other, because their bodies force them to the contact. But in the spiritual spheres it is not so. There, spirit meets spirit alone, and if they stand on different planes they cannot communicate. You may have noticed that Susan is not aware of your presence, though you see and hear her. It is because she dwells upon a higher plane than yourself, and is actually insensible of your contiguity. She neither sees your spirit, nor hears your voice."

"How was it, then, that when we met in the spheres she saw, recognized, and spoke to me?"

"Because, she had come down, on that occasion, from a higher sphere, in obedience to higher orders, that her behaviour might convey some truth of your real position to your mind. When you reach her plane she will be able to communicate with you anywhere. But, when leaving her own spiritual sphere to benefit the denizens of earth, she can only see and hear those who dwell with her in spirit life."

"Why, Mumsey, how bright you look," exclaimed Maddy, as she flung her hat upon a chair. "Who has been here during my absence?"

"Only cousin Ned," replied Ethel, rather consciously.

"Only cousin Ned, you sly Mumsey," cried Maddy, laughing, "we all know what that means. 'Only cousin Ned' will carry you off some day, I expect, if I don't look sharp after you."

"Maddy, dear, don't talk of such a thing yet. It is so horribly soon," remonstrated Ethel.

"Too soon to be happy, my dear?" replied the girl, in a more familiar tone than she had ever assumed towards her step-mother during her father's life-time. "Now, don't go in for any such faddish idea. We've had quite enough misery, you and I, to last a life-time. The sooner we can forget it the better. For my part, I intend to do as I please henceforward."

"Dearest Maddy, you know I love you, and most earnestly wish you to be happy," said Ethel; "but don't be in too great a hurry. You are freed now from all annoyance, and as soon as you come of age you will have your own money, and be quite independent. Take a little time to look about you, dear. If this house is in any way unpleasant to you, tell me, and we will go somewhere else—

abroad, if you fancy it—only take time to think before you settle your final destiny. You know what I mean, dear. I am so afraid that young Mr. Reynolds will draw you into an engagement, or something of the sort, and that you will bind yourself to marry him before you have seen anything of the world, or met other men whom you might, perhaps, like better."

"Now, Mumsey, I thought that was a forbidden subject. You're a darling thing; but you're only my step-mother, you know, and absurdly young for that. I confess I like Will Reynolds. He's an awfully jolly fellow; but I've made no promises as yet, so don't frighten yourself."

"Have you been there this morning, Maddy?"

"Yes; but only to the studio; so don't make a fuss about it. But such a wonderful thing has happened. I cannot understand it at all."

"What is it, dear?"

"Well, Will proposed to take me yesterday morning; but, when I arrived at the studio, I found Rosa Burns there before me; and she was most anxious to be done, as it was for a birthday present for her mother, next week. So Will took us both, separately first; and then, as we were such friends, he said he would take us together. As he took the negative from the camera, I saw him look at it very curiously, and then make a motion as though he would rub out the impression again. I asked him what he had got there, and he said the plate must have been dirty, for it seemed all smudged. He got another, and put it in, with the same result. So, then, he said it was the funniest thing he had ever seen, and, with our permission, he would develop the plates. This morning he asked me to go round and see the result, and it is the most extraordinary thing you ever heard, Mumsey; but, on the photographs he took of me and Rosa, there appear two other figures, standing behind us."

"O, Maddy, you are laughing at me. It is impossible."

"I should have said the same, if I had not seen it. Wilfred gave me one of each of them to bring home. He said that you might be able to solve the mystery. You must understand, Mumsey, that we were quite alone with him, Rosa and I, in his studio—not even an assistant near. Besides, both the figures that have come out are those of women. Here they are," said Maddy, producing them from her bag.

"Mr. Reynolds must have been playing a trick on you, just to see your consternation," said Ethel. "How could any forms but yours have appeared on the plates, unless they were there before he placed them in the camera?"

"I can't answer that question," replied the girl; "but I know that Will was quite as astonished as we were. He says he never heard of such a thing in his life before. There they are," she continued, as she placed the negatives in her step-mother's lap. "The old woman with her hands on Rosa's shoulders, is so like old Mrs. Burns, her grandmother, who died last year, that I could almost swear it is she, or taken from one of her photographs. But who is this bending over me? I cannot recognize it at all. It seems to be a tall, slight woman, with long, loose-flowing hair. Whatever can it all mean, Mumsey? It isn't canny. It half frightens me."

Ethel gazed at the picture for a few seconds in silence; then she suddenly turned pale.

"What is it?" exclaimed Madeline. "Do you know?"

"Know, my dear; how should I know? It is as mysterious to me as to you. But there is a strange familiarity in this figure to me. I suppose it can only be my fancy. But, do you remember your mother, Maddy?"

"Very indistinctly, dear. You know, I was only eight years old when she died, and father never spoke to Gilbert and me of her, or kept her likeness about, or did anything to recall her to our minds. I can just remember that she was very tall and graceful in figure, and her face was generally sad. Poor mother! I daresay she had cause enough. But why do you ask?"

"Because this form—O, it must be only my fancy—seems to remind me of some photographs I once saw in a drawer of your father's writing-table in the library. Have you never seen them, Maddy?"

"Never; you know how disagreeable he was if any one invaded his precincts; and, goodness knows, there was no inducement to do so; and, since his death, the library has had such unpleasant memories for me, that I never go near it. It recalls him and his charming demeanour too vividly."

"I have felt much the same; but I should really like to have a look at those photographs again. Besides, they should, naturally, be in your hands now, since no one can be nearer to your dear mother than yourself and Gillie."

"Ah, dear, *dear* Gillie!" sighed Madeline. "Mumsey, if I ever felt inclined to forgive my father for all his beastly conduct to us (which I don't), the thought of my dear brother would prevent me. I wonder if we shall ever see him again."

"Yes, yes, my dear; we shall. Don't be afraid of that. Cousin Ned has been talking to me about it this morning, and he feels convinced that, as soon as dear Gillie hears of his father's death (as sooner or later he must do), he will come home again. But come with me to the library. I don't believe I should have the nerve to go by myself. The old feeling is so strong upon me still, that I should expect to see the Professor peeping in upon me whilst I was rifling his drawers, and demanding, in that awful voice of his, why I was tampering with his private property."

"Thank goodness; he can never 'pop' in upon any one of us again," cried his daughter. "But I will go and protect you, Mumsey, all the same."

As the ladies left the room, the Professor saw Susan glide after them, and looked inquiringly at John Forest.

"Yes; you can follow them," was the voiceless reply.

"I am more curious to see this photograph than I can say," exclaimed Ethel, as they neared the library door, "and I wonder I have not thought of handing it over to you before."

"*I* don't," replied Madeline. "The wonder would be if any one of us had not avoided everything we could that was likely to remind us of the 'dear departed.'"

"But I have always felt an inexplicable sympathy and affection for the memory of your dear mother," said Ethel.

"A fellow feeling makes us wondrous kind," laughed the girl.

"But you must love her memory, too, dear Maddy."

"Yes; in a measure. She must have been a very unhappy woman, and I pity her. But why did she ever marry such a man as my father? She did us a worse turn than she did herself; for poor

Gilbert and I have the misfortune to have his blood in our veins; whilst in that, she, of course, came off scot-free. But, whatever follies she committed, she must have expurgated them all. To live for ten years with the Professor must have been sufficient to atone for any amount of error."

"Do you hear how your children think and speak of you?" asked John Forest. "Do you comprehend that this is but the beginning of evil, and the opinion Madeline has conceived from your example of man and his capability of wrong-doing will follow her throughout her life?"

"You need not remind me; I comprehend it all," groaned the Professor.

The young women had reached the writing-table by this time and commenced to open the drawers. Most of them were filled with piles of paid bills, notes for the Professor's work, letters from his scientific correspondents, and manuscripts which he had left unfinished behind him. At last, shoved away at the back of one of the drawers, Ethel came upon what she sought—a packet of small, old-fashioned photographs, taken before cabinets were thought of, and in which the Professor's first wife figured in rococo dresses,[23] with inflated skirts.

"What guys," cried Madeline, irreverently, as they came to view. "Can this really be intended for my mother? The faint recollection I have of her doesn't look a bit like this to me; but, then, she was ill, and generally lying on the sofa for some time before she died."

"But, Maddy, don't you see the resemblance?" cried Ethel, excitedly, as she compared the old photographs with the negative impressions the girl had brought home. "It may be my fancy; but I cannot help seeing it. And yet—and yet—*how can it be?*"

"There certainly is a sort of resemblance," acquiesced Madeline; "but, Mumsey, as you say, how can it be? How *could* poor mamma be photographed on the plate with me, when she has been dead for ten years? It is ridiculous. But, then, who is this lady who appears standing by my side, and where did she come from? She

---

[23] Elaborate, tight fitting dress very much a style from the eighteenth century. Some features of the rococo dress reappeared briefly in the nineteenth century.

certainly was not in the studio. It is perfectly maddening to think of."

Susan was standing now close behind Ethel, and, apparently, every now and then, stooping and whispering in her ear. At such moments, Mrs. Aldwyn appeared to become very thoughtful and dreamy."

"Maddy," she said, presently, "there is certainly something very wonderful and mysterious in this business, and which is, at present, perfectly inexplicable to me. But do not let us decide too hastily. A thought has come into my head of some one who may be able to help us to an explanation of it. Do you remember my speaking to you once, long ago, of a friend of mine, Mrs. Blewitt, whom I wished to visit, and was much disappointed because your papa put his veto on it?"

"As he did on every innocent pleasure you desired," replied the girl.

"Well, darling, we need ask no ones permission now, at all events. If you will come back to the drawing-room with me, I will tell you who Mrs. Blewitt is, and why the Professor made object-ions to our acquaintance. Perhaps he was right in acting according to his lights—"

"Which were remarkably small ones," interposed Maddy.

"But we are free agents now, and can judge for ourselves. Bring your dear mother's likenesses with you, as well as Mr. Reynolds' negatives, and I will tell you the strange thought that has come into my head. Do you remember how angry papa was because he over-heard me telling you and Gilbert that spirits were ordained of God to watch over and guide us during our journey through this world?"

"Yes; I remember it perfectly, and how disappointed we were because you were not allowed to tell us any more. But don't, for goodness' sake, Mumsey, tell me that the 'dear departed,' clothed in a sheet, with wings on his back, is to be appointed my guardian angel, because I won't have it. I've had more than enough of him and his guardianship already; and, if I thought he was going to return to this world, I should get a dose of strychnia,[24] and despatch myself to the next. The disappointment would turn my brain."

"I am going to tell you nothing of the sort, you silly girl," replied Ethel, who could not help laughing at the idea, nevertheless; "but let us sit down for a cosy chat, and I will try and explain to you what I mean."

---

[24] Strychnia poisoning was a common method of suicide in the nineteenth century.

- CHAPTER EIGHT -

THE MEDIUM

A s they re-entered the drawing-room, Ethel sat down on the sofa, and Madeline placed herself on a footstool at her feet.
"Now for Mrs. Blewitt," said the girl.

"She was a servant of my mother's, down at Beer, for many years, and only left us to marry James Blewitt," answered Ethel.

"She was always rather a strange girl—uncanny, mother used to call her. She could tell the cards in the most wonderful manner, and everything she foretold through them came true, until the villagers used to ask her to lay them on every occasion, and mother was obliged to forbid her doing so, it became such a nuisance. She had wonderful eyes, too, quite different from those of other people, and was able to foretell if invalids would live or die, and whether the harvest would fail or be fruitful, and all sorts of curious things. I was very young when she lived with us, and they kept the knowledge from me, but I heard the stories afterwards from others. Mother told me, only the other day, that, when I married your papa, Emily (that was her name) wrote and told her that I should be a widow in two years, though how she knew I cannot possibly tell."

"Why didn't your mother tell you of it at the time?" said Maddy. "It would have been such a relief."

"Hush, Maddy. Well, Emily left us, as I said, to marry James Blewitt, Captain Grandison's groom, and they came to London to set up a public house. After awhile, however, they failed, and James had to take another situation, and then I heard, to my surprise, that Emily was laying the cards for people in town, and making quite a lot of money by it."

"Do people pay for that sort of thing? But what is the good?" demanded Maddy.

"I don't know, my dear. I am only telling you what I heard. I wanted to go and see Emily, but your father knew her occupation, and he forbade me doing so, so I was obliged to give up the idea. But it has struck me that she is the very person to explain this mystery to us, if anybody can, and, if you like, we will go and see her this afternoon. I have her address in my desk. I have always kept it in case the Professor should have taken it into his head to leave us alone for a space, and then I should have paid her a visit."

"This is nice," thought the Professor. "My own wife plotting to deceive me during my absence. Can women ever be trusted to be true and faithful?"

"Certainly, if you are true to them and to yourself," replied his guide; "but if you treat them with suspicion, when there is no necessity for it, you will find they are quite clever enough to outwit you."

"But, Mumsey," said Madeline; "how can this woman know anything more than ourselves about this photograph? She never saw or heard of my mother. How can she explain what is really inexplicable?"

"I cannot tell you, Maddy, but I have heard some wonderful accounts of her. She is what is called a clairvoyant, or one who has the gift of second sight. You have heard spiritualism mentioned, haven't you?"

"O, yes, but that is all rubbish," exclaimed the girl, with the audacity of ignorance. "How can it be anything else? No one, with any sense, could really believe that dead people come back to this world again. It is too silly. Besides, I don't believe when we die that anything of us remains. We are buried, and there is an end of us. Papa always said this life ended everything; and, with all his eccentricities and unpleasantness he was a clever man—you will not deny that."

"I know he was, Maddy; but even clever men have been very much mistaken on this point, sometimes. I consider one of the worst things your father ever did, was talking so openly, before his children, of his belief in annihilation. If you believe that, you must disbelieve in God and the Bible. But I feel sure it is not true."

"I don't know why you do not like the idea, Mumsey. I'm sure we have more than enough of this life, without wanting another.

Why, when I die, if I enter another world, I may meet papa there. On that score alone, I prefer to disbelieve in the chance of it. If it is to be, I would rather not know it till it comes."

"Your own child would rather give up the hope of another life than run the risk of meeting you again. Do you make a note of that?" asked John Forest of the Professor. But all the answer he received was conveyed by a groan.

"Never mind, darling," was Ethel's response. "Will you come with me and see my old friend Emily, or not?"

"O, yes, I shall like to go. It will be fun, I expect. But you will never make me believe in spirits, Mumsey, so give up all hope of it."

"I don't believe in them myself, my dear. I know nothing about them, but I should like to show these two photographs to Emily, and hear what she thinks about them."

Accordingly, as soon as they had finished their luncheon, the two young women entered their carriage and ordered it driven to a small row of houses in Bermondsey.[25]

Mrs. Blewitt, who was a very ordinary-looking woman, was rather flustered at first, by the appearance of a grand carriage, with two horses, standing at her door, but as soon as she found the occupants were her dear "Miss Ethel" and her daughter, she was all excitement and delight at the honour of receiving them.

"O, my dear Miss Ethel—Mrs. Aldwyn—I beg your pardon," she cried. "Now, do send your horses away for a bit, and stay and have a cup of tea with me. You won't think it a liberty, my dear, I'm sure; not if you are the same dear young lady as I knew down at Beer, for I've hungered and thirsted for a sight of you, ever since you came up to London, and sadly disappointed that I never saw you."

"Well, it has not been entirely my fault, Emily, that I have not been before, but I have not forgotten you all the same. Maddy, dear, tell James to have the horses put up for a couple of hours, and call here again for us at six o'clock. That will give us time for a

---

[25] Bermondsey is on the south bank of the River Thames. In the nineteenth century it was largely a slum area with immigrant housing and a working dock.

nice, long chat."

"And so you're a widow, my dear," commenced Mrs. Blewitt, as soon as they had settled down together, "I ought to have condoled with you before this."

"How did you hear of it, Emily? Has mother written to you, or did you read it in the papers?"

"Neither the one nor the other, Miss Ethel. Your dear mamma has too much to do with her large family to have time to write to me, and, as for papers, I don't see one in a blue moon. No, it was through the cards I saw it—though there's been some one as belongs to you, or wants to get speech of you, hanging about me for a long time past."

"Some one hanging about you, Emily. What do you mean?"

"A spirit, my dear," replied Mrs. Blewitt, readily. "I don't think she's of your blood, but I know she wants to speak to you. She's worritted me for a long time past, and it's no good my telling her to go away, for she won't, and that's just the truth."

"You don't really believe, Emily, that spirits can come back to earth and talk to mortals, do you?" said Ethel, smiling.

"Don't believe it, my dear?" replied the woman, "Well, I should be a greater fool than I take myself for if I didn't believe it. How can I help believing it, when they're about and around me day and night? Have you never heard," she continued, in a lower voice, "how I makes my living now-a-days?"

"I have heard that you are, or fancy yourself to be, what people call a medium," replied Mrs. Aldwyn; "but as I know nothing about it, I have not known what to believe."

"Ah, it's a pity you don't know more about it, Miss Ethel, and, perhaps, I may have the happiness of teaching you what you don't know. Don't you believe any of them parsons, or other fellers, as think themselves mighty clever, and tell you there's nothing in it. For there's *everything* in it. There's life and health and happiness in it, and in nothing else. If you knew what I know (though I'm only a poor, ignorant woman), and felt as I feel, you wouldn't fear death no more than you do your bed."

"Tell us about it, Emily," said Ethel, drawing closer to her. "Both my step-daughter and I are interested in the subject, and would like to hear all you have to say."

"All I have to say," repeated Mrs. Blewitt; "why, that would take more time than you would give to it, Miss Ethel. But it's Bible truth, that the spirits of the dead can return. They're about me day and night."

"It's very 'creepy' to think of," said Mrs. Aldwyn, with a shudder; "don't they frighten you awfully, Emily? I think I should die if I were to see one."

"O, no, my dear, you wouldn't. You'd come to look upon them as your best friends—as, indeed, they are."

"But how did you find out first that you were a medium, Emily? You were not one down at Beer."

"O, yes, Miss Ethel, I must have been, but I was too ignorant to perceive it. But when I settled in London, I got mixed up with a family of spiritualists and used to 'sit' with them; and one evening, all of a sudden, I was controlled, and it has continued ever since."

"What do you mean by 'controlled,' Emily?"

"I lost my consciousness, and some one else took possession of my body and spoke through my mouth, Miss Ethel. But it wasn't that fact, alone; it was that I spoke of things and people that I had never heard of or seen, but which those present knew to be truths. My principal control now, Doctor Abernethy, will write pre-scriptions, in Latin, for the sick, and cure them in a most marvellous manner, whilst I am fast asleep. And you know, Miss Ethel, that if I wasn't, I never could write Latin, nor show any knowledge of medicine—could I, now?"

"No, it all seems very wonderful. And you really make money by it?"

"Well, we mustn't talk too loud of that," replied Emily, "for whilst the law is against it, I am apt to get into trouble if it should get about. But I have a large connection now, and, of course, the ladies and gentlemen who come here to consult my guides, leave a little recognition of my services behind them. And since we failed, I'm sure I don't know what James and me would have done without it, sometimes."

"Well, you have interested me very much, Emily, and I came here this afternoon to see if you could explain away a little mystery for us."

Ethel then produced the photographs of the Professor's first wife, with the negatives taken by Mr. Reynolds, and told her the story of them. Emily looked at the pictures for some time in silence; then she exclaimed, suddenly:

"I know who the lady is. It is the same as has worritted me for so long. Wait a bit and I'll give you her name, she's telling it to me now; Su—Susan—yes, that's it, but it's the young lady she wants, Miss Ethel, not you. Well, this is the curiousest thing as I've ever seen. This is her spirit photograph. Aye, you may stare, ladies, but it's a commoner thing than you think of. I've been taken with them several times myself. By the way, Miss Ethel, do you mind my old father who used to work for Captain Grandison—Isaac Bond—many a ride he's given you before him when he was taking his horses down to water."

"Of course I remember him, Emily. Didn't I knit him a scarlet woollen comforter,[26] the first piece of knitting I ever did, and took it to him when he was lying in bed with the rheumatism?"

"Of course you did, and I'm glad of it, for you will have no difficulty in recognizing his features. There, Miss, what do you think of that," exclaimed Mrs. Blewitt, as she produced a photograph of herself and her husband, sitting lovingly on a sofa together, whilst behind them stood the figure of an old labourer, in a smock frock.

"O, Emily, this is very, very wonderful; how well I remember your old father's shock of grey hair, and the way he used to lean with both hands on his thick staff. But do you mean to tell me he did not stand for this picture with Blewitt and you?"

"O, father stood for it, sure enough, Miss Ethel; but he's been passed over for five years and more, and that photo was only taken last December. I sent one home to mother and she cried with joy, for she hadn't a single likeness to remind her of the old man. It made a spiritualist of mother at once, that picture did, though she had been dead set against it before, but there was no going against her own eyes."

---

[26] A woollen comforter is a type of blanket, very much like a quilt.

"And you really think—" said Mrs. Aldwyn, still fingering the likenesses of Susan—"that—that—this portrait was—"

She halted, for she didn't know what to say. The astonishment was too great to permit her utterance.

"I don't *think*, Miss Ethel, I'm sure that the lady, who's been round about me for so long, is the same that is in that photograph; and if so be, as you say, she's passed over to the spirit world, why, then, that's a spirit photograph, and nothing else. May I be so bold as to ask who took it?"

"A young photographer named Reynolds," answered Ethel. "He was as astonished as we were at what had occurred, and could give no explanation of it."

"Well, he must be a powerful medium, whoever he is, and may make his fortune if he chooses. No one could produce that photograph who wasn't a first-class medium."

"Do you mean," asked Maddy, speaking for the first time, "that he will have spirits and ghosts and those sorts of things always about him? Because he is not a spiritualist. He doesn't believe in it at all."

"That won't signify, Miss, if so be as he has the gift. The spirits will find him out, sure enough. He won't be able to keep out of it. If they want his work, he'll have to give it them."

Maddy drew nearer to Ethel, and got hold of her hand.

"If that's the case, he won't see much more of me," she whispered, with a scared face. "Why, he might take it in his head to come back some day and be photographed. The risk is too great. I shall never sit to Will Reynolds again."

"You foolish girl," said Ethel, "you are talking of a matter of which you know positively nothing."

"And believe less," said Madeline.

"Then why make such irrelevant remarks? For my own part, I think I should dearly like to inquire further into it, if Emily, here, can promise me that I shall not be frightened."

"My dear lady, there is nothing to be frightened at. My other control, 'Margaret,' is such a pure, gentle spirit, I am sure you will love her. Well, if you fancy it, suppose you let me give you and the young lady a cup of tea, and then we will go up into my private room and I will have the pleasure of giving you a séance.

"O, Emily, you *are* good," exclaimed Ethel, "I should like it above all things. Wouldn't you, Maddy?"

"I don't know," replied that young lady. "If Mrs. Blewitt will promise not to bring back papa."

"My dear Miss Aldwyn, I have not the power to *bring* back any one, but should there be anybody you particularly do not wish to speak to, I feel sure your own guardian spirit will keep him away."

Mrs. Blewitt then rose to make her preparations for tea, and Maddy cuddled up to her stepmother.

"Do you know, Mumsey, I feel very much inclined to run away. It makes me half afraid. I feel as if something terrible were going to happen. Don't you?"

"On the contrary, I am only very curious, Maddy. But I must say, Emily's evident belief in spiritualism has made me think there must be something in it. She was always such a simple, straightforward, honest woman. My mother used to say she was too honest. She put away every scrap of paper, or needleful of thread, she found about the house. And surely she could never make money by it, if it were all humbug. People would find her out and expose her. I am most anxious to see her under control."

"What will she do? Will she have fits, or things?" asked Maddy.

"I hope not, dear," said Ethel; and, as Mrs. Blewitt returned with the tea-tray, she told her what Maddy had said.

"I shall do nothing to frighten you, my dear young lady," she replied; "but, drink your tea first, and then you will say I have kept my word. And how long is it since you went down to Beer, Miss Ethel? And how is your dear mamma? And is it long since you heard from home?"

"No, indeed, Emily; mother is a capital correspondent, and writes to me regularly once a week. And Miss Gussie was married last summer, and has such a sweet, little baby. And my sister, Carrie, is engaged, too—to a young clergyman—and father and mother are so pleased about it. I was down at Beer, this spring, for a whole month. It was delightful to see the old place again, and all my brothers and sisters. Your last baby, Master Bobby, has grown such a fine fellow, six years old last birthday, and rides his pony like a little man. Mother spoils him, of course; but then he is the baby, you see, and, I suppose, will always remain so, in her eyes."

"And have you no baby of your own, Miss Ethel?" asked Mrs. Blewitt.

"No; thank God," was on the tip of Ethel's tongue; but she changed the words in time to "No, Emily, and I'm not sorry for it. I never cared much for children, you know, and I have two big ones—this young lady here, and my step-son, who is at sea, But, if you are ready, I think we had better get our little business over; for I ordered the carriage to call for us at six, and the time must be getting on."

"Very good, my dear. If you will accompany me to my own room, we will sit at once."

Mrs. Blewitt lit a candle as she spoke, and preceded the ladies up-stairs. Maddy hung back, and would not have had the courage to go at all, had not Ethel grasped her hand firmly and drawn her after her.

Emily's sitting-room was a tiny apartment, containing only a small table and three or four chairs; but she accounted for the paucity of furniture by saying that, as a rule, she never sat for more than one person at a time.

"You see, Miss Ethel, 'Margaret' cannot speak as freely as she likes if she sees more than one sitter; but, with you and Miss Aldwyn, it is, of course, different. You can have no secrets from each other; but, with most people, it is quite another thing. O, I have had the awkwardest things said as ever you heard on—wives' secrets coming out before their husbands, and *vice versa*, as Master Richard used to say at home. I don't know anything about them, of course, being fast asleep; but I've found ladies and gentlemen in fine rages when I waked up. So, now, I make it a rule to see only one at a time; and they are often thankful for it afterwards, and come and tell me so. But now we will be quiet for a few minutes, if you please, and see if any of our friends are about."

Saying which, Mrs. Blewitt closed her eyes, and, in another moment, her head fell forward on her bosom, and she was asleep. But the sleep was evidently not a natural one. She sat quiet for a little while, and then began to moan and gasp, as if speaking were a terrible effort to her. Her actions frightened Maddy, who was with difficulty prevented from running out of the room.

"No, Maddy, now we are here, do be sensible,' urged Ethel. "You heard Emily say that nothing would harm us, so let us sit it out to the end. How silly we should look if we ran away and left poor Emily, after all her kindness to us, to wake up and find herself alone. Hark! she is going to speak."

Mrs. Blewitt sat bolt upright in her chair, and regarded the two nervous women with an amused air.

"Do I alarm you?" she asked.

Ethel did not know what to answer, or who to address. Was this Emily who spoke to her, or a stranger? So she said, timidly:

"Not precisely; but we don't know who you are. Are you Emily?"

"O, no; the medium has gone far away, and will not return till we have done with her. I am 'Margaret,' of whom you heard her speak."

"But what is your other name? There are so many Margarets in the world," said Ethel.

"My other name would carry no significance with it for you. I was a very humble body whilst on this earth, but all my friends here call me 'Margaret.' You are trembling. You are frightened. Is it because I speak to you?"

"No; but it is all so strange to us. We are not accustomed to it. We have been taught that spirits cannot communicate with mortals—that it is folly to think so—and, by some, that there is no spirit at all, but that when the body dies all dies with it."

"They must have been very ignorant and silly people who tried to make you believe that. Why, the spirit lives for ever and ever. You must believe it when I tell you, because I am a spirit who left this earth more than two hundred years ago."

"Is that possible? But why do you come back then? Why don't you stay in heaven, or wherever you may be at present?"

"I come back to try and do good to my fellow mortals, as I am attempting to-night with you. You both need spirit guidance very much, especially this young lady. It was no accident that brought her here to-night. A spirit who loves her and watches over her was the means of her coming. She tried to speak to her just now, but could not manage it; so she sent me instead, but she will try again later on."

"Who is this spirit who cares for me?" demanded Madeline, eagerly.

"Be patient, and she will tell you, herself. She would not like me to forestall her. She has been trying for so long to communicate with you. But you need not fear her. She loves you very dearly, and has done so from your birth."

Then she turned to Ethel, and said, with an amused air:

"And so you have pledged yourself to marry again? Your late experience has not frightened you altogether from entering the holy state."

Madeline looked surprised, and whispered, "Mumsey, is that true?" and Ethel coloured to her eyes, and asked Margaret how she came to know it.

"Why, I can read it in your mind. It was only this morning that it occurred. Am I not right? But I congratulate you. You have made a wise and good choice this time, and chosen a man who will make you very happy. I see you in the future, with his children round you, blessing God, not only for the gift of him and his love, but also for the trials which you passed through before you became his wife. The remembrance of them will make your future all the happier from the contrast."

"Cousin Ned, Mumsey, of course?" whispered Maddy.

"O, my dear child, yes; but, however she came to find it out, I cannot imagine. It is more than wonderful. It is magical."

"O, no," said the spirit; "don't let any such false conceptions enter your head. There is nothing magical about me. I am only a woman, like yourself. But, when you pass over to the spiritual spheres, and leave the evil influences of earth behind you—the deceit and fraud, the lying and slander, the hypocrisy and ill-nature—you will find all the senses which the Creator intended you, from the beginning, to enjoy in your life, but which have been deadened and over-clouded by sin and disease, wonderfully strengthened and developed, so that you will be able to read each other's minds, and anticipate what is going to happen to you. This is not magic; it is Spiritualism."

"Have you anything to tell *me?*" asked Maddy, who was beginning to take a great interest in the proceedings. "Can you see anything in the future for me?"

"Yes, indeed; but not until you have passed through a hard trial. You are on the brink of a great danger, that threatens to overshadow your whole life. Your senses are fascinated, in some way, by a friend (if I can call him such) who courts you only for the advantages he may gain through you. He has a pleasant manner, though rather a rough and unpolished one; and, if you link your fate with his, he will make you very unhappy, and gradually alienate you from all your present friends. If you search your heart honestly, you will find that you do not really care for this person. At times, all his deficiencies burst upon your mind, and make you disgusted with him and yourself; but the old glamour returns when you meet again. This is not love; it is animal magnetism, a force of which the inhabitants of earth know far too little, or they would not mistake it for a higher feeling. Shall I tell you how you may always recognize if the sentiment you have conceived for one of the opposite sex is love, or not?"

"Yes, do," cried Maddy. "It may be useful."

"If, when you feel that a man has so high a notion of honour, and so nice a balance of equity, and so great a horror of all that is low and mean and false, that, strive as you may, you will never be able to reach his standard of right; when, joined to this belief, you feel as if you could not live except under his guidance and mastery, then you may say to yourself that you love him as a woman should love a man, and trust your future fearlessly to his care."

"O, but where are such men to be found?" said the girl. "They don't live in the world nowadays."

"I think some do," said Ethel, softly. "I think Ned is just one of those men. Am I not right, Margaret?"

But Margaret seemed to have flown away. Mrs. Blewitt was reclining in her chair, with her eyes fast closed and her natural expression on her face.

- CHAPTER NINE -

SUSAN SPEAKS TO MADELINE

"She has fallen asleep again. Do you think any one else will come?" demanded Madeline of her stepmother.

"I do not know; but we had better keep quiet and see what happens. You are not frightened any longer, dear, are you?"

"No, not at all; but so marvellously interested. Do you know, I feel already that I shall never rest till I have solved this mystery to the bottom. I must prove if it is false, or true. If true, how dare people say it is wrong?"

"How dare they, indeed?" replied Mrs. Blewitt, as she sat up again in her chair. "But they will have to answer for it by and by. Many a poor wretch is treading the paths of purgatory now, for having led his brethren astray in this particular."

Then she held out her arms to Madeline, and murmured: "My child; my dear child."

"O, Mumsey," cried the girl, half frightened; "who is it?"

"Ask her, dear," cried Ethel, gently.

"Don't you know me?" said the spirit. "Is not my voice an echo of one you listened to long ago? Madeline, my daughter! I am your mother."

The girl did not know what to do. If this really were her mother—if she had been sure of it—she would have flown into her arms; but it was all so strange—they were Mrs. Blewitt's arms—and she held back uncertainly.

"O, I remember you, and I love you," she exclaimed; "at least, I love my mother's memory; but how am I to know that you are she? Give me some proof. Tell me something that no one can know but our two selves—that Mrs. Blewitt is not aware of."

"It is only natural that you should require some proof. But it is so long since we parted, and I have not been able to get near you till lately. But I have heard you mention the unhappy man you call your father. Madeline, you must not speak of him as you do. If you knew the torments he is undergoing, the hell in which he lives; not the practical hell you have been taught to believe in, but one far worse, a hell of unfulfilled desires and racking remorse, 'where the worm dieth not, and the fire is not quenched,'[27] you would pray, night and day, that his misery might be abated, and that you, who inherit much of his temperament, may escape so terrible a fate."

"Is papa so very unhappy, then?" inquired Madeline, in an awed voice.

"No words of mine could depict the agony of mind he is suffering at the present moment—an agony he has brought completely on himself. He might have made life bright and happy for himself and all around him; but he chose to indulge his own selfish disposition, and so he has to expiate it to the last item. But it is not for his daughter to execrate his memory. He sinned, doubtless sinned heavily, for the greatest sins we can commit in this world are those which injure our fellow creatures; but he is gone—he can never hurt you more. Be merciful, then, as you hope for mercy, or you may bring a like punishment on your own head."

"Mother—if you are my mother—where did you ever hear me speak against papa?" said Madeline.

"I have heard you many times, both before his death and since, but one instance will suffice to prove that what I say is true. *Who* was it who, on the day which preceded his sudden death, made a profound curtsy behind his back, as soon as he had quitted the luncheon room, and said: 'O, you nice, dear, careful father! You ought to have a statue erected to you, you ought. Why, you haven't as much feeling for your own children as a cat has for her kittens. If I thought I could ever behave like that to mine, I would go and hang myself before I had any'?"

By this time Madeline had hidden her face in Ethel's lap.

"O, Mumsey, Mumsey," she cried, "it is all true, every word of it."

"Of course it is all true, dear," replied Susan. "Did you suppose

---

[27] Mark chpt. 9, v. 48 'Where their worm dieth not, and the fire is not quenched.'

that I had been in the other world all this time, ten long years, and never come back to see my dear Gilbert or you? Should I have been contented, whilst on earth, to have neglected you for so long? Why, the first boon I asked was to be allowed to return to my dear children. Only, I have never been able to get so near to you as now. *His* influence kept me at a distance."

"But if you come, may not he?" asked Maddy, presently.

"No, no, not for a long time, at least; certainly not until you have learned to think far more tenderly and compassionately of his past errors. Your controlling spirits would not let him approach you. *I* would not. He cannot stand on the same plane as myself, nor can he communicate with me; but my very presence would prevent his coming too near. Do not be afraid, my darling; your father shall not be permitted to annoy you."

At these words, the Professor, who had been present during the whole of the interview, became very indignant. Not to be allowed to approach his own children, indeed! Why should Susan be permitted to manifest herself, speaking to them openly of his faults and condition, and setting their minds against him, whilst he stood by and had not a word to say. He was springing forward to take possession of the medium in his turn, when he found his feet glued to the spot whereon he stood. No efforts of his could un-loose them. They were chained to the ground.

"What does this mean?" he asked, angrily.

"Simply, that you are to stay where you are," replied John Forest.

"Why should Susan be able to address Madeline, and not I?"

"Because she has received the permission of the Almighty, and you have not," was the answer. "If you spoke to Madeline you would undo all the good we hope to effect through Susan. You heard the distaste, nay, the fear, with which she anticipated your return. One word from you at this crisis would change the current of her life. It would so horrify her with Spiritualism that she would never seek it again."

"Shall I never be able to address her or my son?"

"Perhaps; it depends upon yourself. At present, you would do them the greatest harm. Let the merciful years roll over the memories you have left behind you. They do not smell sweet at this moment."

"O, mother! I believe you *are* my mother," Maddy was saying, when he listened to her voice next; "and I am so very glad that I came here to meet you again."

"You did not come, my dear child; you were brought," returned the spirit. "It was I, myself, who accompanied you from Ethel's house to this one. And now, one word to her. Thank you a thousand times, my dear sister, for the love and consideration you have shown to my children. It has not been unnoted; it will not be forgotten, but redound in blessings on the heads of your own. But I must go now. The power is exhausted."

"One moment, mother," exclaimed Madeline, who had sunk on her knees, and clasped her arms round the form of the medium. "About that photograph!—was it—can it have been you?"

"Assuredly it was I, my child. Who else could have imprinted my features on the camera, when, as you know, the only likenesses ever taken of me were locked away in your father's writing-table? I did that as a test, as something that should startle you and arrest your attention, as nothing else could have done. People might have talked to you of Spiritualism (as they did to your poor father) and only made you more obstinately resolved to believe nothing but what you chose; but I knew the sight of my features would make you pause and think. And I have been successful."

"You have, indeed," replied Madeline, seriously. "I feel to-day as I have never felt before."

"Good-by, good-by, dearest child," said Susan, as, with a solemn kiss on her daughter's forehead, she passed away again, and Mrs. Blewitt came back to earth life. She yawned once or twice, and then opened her eyes, smiling.

"I hope you have had a good sitting, Miss Ethel," she said. "Has any one been here?"

"O, yes, Emily," replied Ethel. "We have been deeply interested; but I do not feel as if I could speak of it yet. It is all so new and wonderful to me."

Then she glanced at Madeline, and saw that she was crying.

"Don't speak to me," said the girl, as she saw a question hovering on the lips of her stepmother. "I cannot help it. Please let me recover by myself."

Ethel and Mrs. Blewitt took the hint, and by the time the carriage called for them the girl was composed enough to return home.

"My daughter and wife complain that I did not direct them aright, with regard to the reality of another life," grumbled the Professor; "but how could I teach them that which I did not know myself? I received no evidences of another life—no spirits took the trouble to come back and teach me. How then am I to blame for their condition of mind?"

"You are infinitely to blame," was the reply; "in fact you are the *only* one to blame. You not only kept others from them, who might have shown them the truth, but you took no steps to find it out for yourself. Because you could find nothing in your gross carnality to prove you had a soul, you jumped to the conclusion that nobody had a soul, and were content to deny the existence of another world, because you had never taken the trouble to inquire whether there was one or not. Had your children entered on spirit life as ignorant as you left them, it would not have been accounted to *them* for evil, but your purgatory would have been increased a hundred-fold."

"Is there any way by which such a possibility may be averted now?" inquired the Professor.

"Did I not tell you yesterday that our lives can be atoned for, by doing them over again? Every sin is forgivable in the eyes of the Almighty Spirit, but every sin must be atoned for. When you have made a mistake, rectify it."

"How can we rectify what is past and gone?"

"By inducing others not to do the same. Every sin prevented is a grace gained. Do you see that wretched-looking woman walking in front of us, with a miserable, starved infant hidden under her ragged shawl? Can you read her thoughts?"

"I can. She thinks how much better it would be to drown herself and the child, than to continue the life of starvation and brutality she is now living. Is she not right? Would it not be better for them to be in the spirit world?"

"Perhaps, but they would not find themselves there. The Almighty has appointed a certain length of existence for every human creature, and, if they cut it short for themselves, they still have to spend it on this earth, wandering about, as you are doing, neither fit for one place or the other. Do you see the spirit who follows in her wake?"

"Yes. Is she a relation, or her guardian angel?"

"Neither. She is a poor creature who committed the same crime: for ingratitude against God is the greatest crime of which a mortal can be guilty. She is earth-bound, in consequence, until she has expiated her error by preventing another creature from committing the same. A life gained will atone for the life she took away. If she can prevent that woman from drowning her baby and herself, as she did whilst on earth, she will be able to plead the rescued lives before God's throne, and He will break off the bands that chain her to the earth sphere."

"And what then?" demanded the Professor.

"The poor spirit will be free to rise and progress. Cannot you perceive the drowned infant is still in her arms? She has had to carry it ever since she took its little life away. It is a constant reproach to her. When, by her influence, she has saved another baby's life, she will be allowed to hand hers over to the care of a sister spirit, and free to forget the unhappy past. Are you beginning to understand how evenly and justly the divine penances work?"

"Yes, but what are these animals that cling so persistently about my feet wherever I go? I do not like animals—I never did—is that a sin? But why should these follow me so persistently?"

"Do you not recognize them? They evidently know you. I think the poor brutes had reason to do so. These are the spirits of the dumb brutes whom you tortured in the name of science. These are the dogs, and rabbits, and cats which you vivisected for your own curiosity, and who died agonizing, lingering deaths under your cruel hands."

"But surely, science must be pursued, even if a few wretched mongrels and cats, of no value to anybody, should have to suffer in its interests."

"You will not find it so, I am afraid. God, who made these

creatures for our pleasure and our use, never intended them to minister to our discoveries, in science or anything else, by means of horrors too terrible to think of. All the long, weary hours of acute pain under which you kept these helpless creatures of God, in order that you might watch their hearts beating, or the various parts of their organism working, have been reckoned up against you, and the animals themselves are ordained to accompany you throughout the hell you have created for yourself, till your own tortures will have so accumulated that you would be thankful to exchange them for those you made them suffer—aye, even to have your head and body laid out and secured on the vivisecting table, as theirs were, whilst all your nerves and most of the delicate portions of your system are mutilated by the dissecting knife. You will find there are two meanings to the text. 'Inasmuch as you have done it unto the least of these my brethren, you have done it unto me.'[28] God, who does not let even a sparrow fall to the ground without His knowledge, will not forget the tortured cries and moans of His helpless animals. No, it is useless for you to try to kick them away. You can no longer harm them, and they are under God's orders, and not yours. Be thankful if you are not condemned to go through what you made them suffer."

"The prospect you hold out is a pleasant one," said the Professor, who was trembling with apprehension.

"It is not intended to be so," replied John Forest, with unintentional satire. "You have not lived the sort of life that commands a pleasant prospect. You men on earth do not know the value of love, nor the consequences of a want of it. I have seen a little, ignorant spirit, who came into our world with all the lying and thieving propensities with which she had been reared from birth, who received her right of progress as soon as she entered the spiritual gates. Why? Because she had loved dumb animals, and shared her mouldy crusts with the mangy mongrels in the gutter, and her bits of rusty bacon with the cats from the house-tops. 'And it was accounted unto her for righteousness.' Do you understand me? Come, we had better be moving on, and you can

---

[28] Matthew chpt 25, v. 40.

bring your little troop of vivisected animals with you. They can inconvenience no one, and, thank the good God, they will never suffer any more. It is your turn now to do that for them, and, perhaps, they would like to see it, and that is why they follow you. It can hardly be from love."

- CHAPTER TEN -

MESSRS. BUNSTER AND ROBSON CALL

The next morning, Mrs. Aldwyn was smiling furtively to herself, over the contents of two letters which she had received through the post, when her stepdaughter entered the room.

"What is the joke, Mumsey?" she asked; "what makes you smile?"

"Nothing in particular, dear; only these two old fogies, Mr. Bunster and Mr. Robson, have both written, desiring to see me on 'particular business.' Whatever can it be?"

"Proposals, evidently. You'll have to make up your mind before this evening, whether you will be Mrs. Bunster or Mrs. Robson."

"Maddy, you silly girl, you know my mind is made up already. But where are you going so early?"—seeing that the girl was attired for walking—"Not to Mr. Reynolds' studio, I hope?"

"No, dear, nothing of the kind; so don't alarm yourself. I am bound in quite an opposite direction."

"I was in hopes you would have supported me under the trying occasion before me."

"O, you will manage very well alone. By the way, how do you know the old gentlemen, or, at all events, one of them, is not coming to offer me his hand? Fancy, if you and I could lead the pair up to the hymeneal altar[29] on the same day. Wouldn't it be romantic? Whom should we ask to be best men? Methuselah[30] is dead, poor dear, or he would have done nicely for one; so is old

---

[29] In Greek mythology Hymen was the god of marriage.
[30] Methuselah is the oldest person whose age is given the Bible, (as 969 years). The name is now synonymous with someone of great age. Genesis, chpt 5, v. 25-27: 'And Methuselah lived an hundred eighty and seven years, and begat Lamech: And Methuselah lived after he begat Lamech seven hundred eighty and two years, and begat sons and daughters: And all the days of Methuselah were nine hundred sixty nine years and he died.'

Parr. But I spotted a couple of centenarians in the *Daily Telegraph* [31] the other day, and we might rout them up, if necessary."

"If you go on any more in this mad strain, Maddy, I shall laugh in the respectable old gentlemen's faces. Do be quiet, and leave me to myself. By the way, where are you going?"

"You shall hear if you will be good and promise not to prevent me. I am going to see Mrs. Blewitt again. I made an arrangement to call this morning, before we parted last night."

"Madeline! you do surprise me. I thought you had such an inherent disbelief in all things supernatural."

"So I had, but how can I disbelieve this? If it is not my mother who spoke through her yesterday, it must be some one who knows all about us, and how can Mrs. Blewitt do so? Mumsey, what happened has made a tremendous impression on me. I can't get it out of my head. I have been thinking of it half the night. You will not try to prevent my visiting Mrs. Blewitt, will you? I want to go again and again, until I have solved the mystery, one way or the other."

"Of course, I shall not attempt any such thing, dearest; but Bermondsey is not a nice place for a young lady to be walking in alone. If you go, you must either take the carriage or Lotsom with you. But I should prefer the carriage, for I do not know what Emily would do with Lotsom while she was engaged with you, and we don't want all the servants' hall discussing our doings, do we?"

"Certainly not. But won't you want the carriage yourself this morning?"

"No, dear. You forget my two old gentlemen are coming to see me. One proposes to be here at eleven, the other at twelve. Such unearthly hours to pay visits. What can they be thinking of?"

"O, I daresay they have some important engagements for the afternoon; a lecture on the 'Nebulæ in the Moon,' or a treatise on the 'Nervous Organization of Frogs'—some of the delightful subjects papa was wrapt up in, and which caused his family circle to be so harmonious."

"Maddy, remember what your mother said to you, and leave

---

[31] The *Daily Telegraph* was established in 1855, its first editor was Thornton Leigh Hunt.

papa's fads alone. If things had ended with them, all would have been right enough. Ring, and order the carriage, dear. It will be round in ten minutes, and then I shall feel easy about you."

Having done as she was told, Madeline asked:

"Mumsey, do you think my mother could tell me where Gillie is, and if we shall see him home again soon?"

"I think it very likely; for, if she can watch over one of her children, surely she would do so for the other. Besides, if I remember rightly, she mentioned Gillie's name with yours. Yes, do ask her, Maddy. It would be such a relief to know the dear boy was safe and well."

The carriage being now announced, the girl, after having affectionately embraced her stepmother, ran off with a face beaming with hope and expectation, whilst Ethel turned her thoughts towards her intended guests.

The Professor was also very much exercised in his mind, as to what his old friends could possibly have to say to his widow. He had left them each a handsome remembrance in his will, consisting of a set of his own works on science, which, as he had told his father, were accepted (at all events, in his own opinion) as unquestionable authority. Perhaps Robson and Bunster had been too delicate to intrude on the widow's supposed grief before, and were coming to offer their condolences on the loss to science of such a luminary as himself. He trusted that Ethel would receive them with becoming dignity, and not let them guess that she revered his memory so little as to have already engaged herself to marry another man. He watched her go up to the drawing-room mirror as the hour of eleven drew near, and pass her fingers through the fluffy curls on her forehead, and smooth down the pleats of her black dress. As the clock struck, Mr. Bunster was announced.

The Professor craned his neck eagerly to catch the first glimpse of his old crony. Bunster was a short, stout, little man of about sixty, with a preponderance of stomach, and a fussy, nervous manner, when with ladies, not unlike the immortal Pickwick.[32] He

---

[32] Charles Dickens's *Posthumous Papers of the Pickwick Club* ran from 1836-1837.

entered the room, wiping his face with his handkerchief, and in a suit of light tweed, with a blue tie.

"I am surprised that Bunster has not even put on a crape band round his hat for me," observed the Professor. "I thought it was considered *comme il faut* to do so, when you received a legacy from a friend."

"Wait and hear what his errand may be before you condemn him," replied John Forest; "he may have some good reason for dressing gaily. Mourning is not worn for so long now as it used to be."

"To be sure. I forgot that," said the Professor.

"How are you, Mr. Bunster?" said Ethel, as she advanced to receive him.

"Quite well, my dear lady, and I hope I see you the same. What a charming day it is, to be sure. Have you been out?"

"Not yet. You timed your visit so early that I thought I had better remain in, for fear of missing you. But will you not be seated?"

"I trust I did not incommode you by naming so early an hour," said Mr. Bunster, as he subsided into a chair. "But I had an especial reason for wishing to see you alone—before the giddy throng of fashion had claimed you for its own."

"O, Mr. Bunster, you mustn't talk of fashion to me. I have been only three months a widow, remember."

"Three months!" exclaimed Bunster, "they have seemed like three years to me."

"Have you really missed your old friend so much as that?" asked Ethel, sympathetically.

"My old friend! Do you mean the Professor? Well, of course, we were friends in a sense—all persons who are interested in the same pursuits cling together. Your late husband, Mrs. Aldwyn, and I were associated in scientific work—and that naturally induced an intimacy—but as for friendship, well, if you will permit me to say so, the bright, particular star that drew me so constantly to this abode was—not the Professor so much as a certain charming lady who presided over it."

"Complimenting my wife. How dare he?" commenced the

Professor.

"O, you will find men are very daring, now that you are out of the way," replied his guide.

"And why should they not be? She is a woman: therefore, to be wooed. She is a woman: therefore, to be won. Don't forget that you are looking at your widow—not your wife."

The Professor swore between his teeth.

"Don't do that, it's foolish," said John Forest. "Every word you say now is noted down, and will be taken as evidence against you."

"O, that is a very pretty compliment," said Ethel, who was already beginning to find it difficult to keep her countenance, with the memory of Madeline's words before her.

"No compliment, I assure you, my dear lady, but the solemn truth," replied Bunster. "No one envied the Professor, during his life-time, more than your humble servant, and no one would—ahem," concluded Mr. Bunster, with a nervous cough.

"I fear you must have taken cold," remarked Ethel; "let me offer you a jujube. Do you like them? Maddy and I think they are lovely. We are always eating them. Our confectioner's bill is something cruel."

"Ah, you love sweets. You must let me send you some. Do you like American candies? There is a shop in Regent street that is quite famous for them. Have you ever tasted candied violets?"

"No, no, Mr. Bunster, I cannot possibly allow you to think of providing our sugary wants. You don't know what you are proposing. You would be ruined in a fortnight. Madeline and I are insatiable. We gormandize sweets all day long."

"Then you would make me happy all day long. Ah, you do not know what bliss it would be for me if I could provide for your every want, dear Mrs. Aldwyn. And it would take you some time to get through my income. I am not dependent on my profession for a living. I inherited an ample fortune from my parents, and I have never wasted it yet on wife or child. As I stand (or I should rather say, as I sit) before you, you view me wholly without incumbrances, or vicious tastes; and, in these days of extravagance and reckless marriages, I consider, dear Mrs. Aldwyn, that that is no mean credential in a man."

"O, certainly not. It is very nice and satisfactory," said Ethel, who did not know what to say.

"Then, will you take me, dearest Mrs. Aldwyn, for your own?" exclaimed Mr. Bunster, falling on one knee before her. "Will you make me the happiest man in England, by accepting my fortune—eight hundred a year in British consols, and all of it would be settled unconditionally on yourself in the event of my demise—and the homage of my life? Will you—of course after the necessary time that custom demands shall have elapsed—become Mrs. Bunster?"

Ethel looked at the prostrate old gentleman for a minute in surprise, and then, feeling more shame than anything else for the folly of which he was guilty, she implored him to get up.

"Do, please, Mr. Bunster," she kept on saying. "Suppose James should come in for anything, it would look so dreadful—so ridiculous—"

"Ridiculous, Mrs. Aldwyn!" exclaimed Bunster, taking offense at once. "I don't consider that is the proper term to apply to the situation. What is there ridiculous in a gentleman making an honourable offer of marriage to the lady of his choice, in the position which has been recognized as the most respectful one from time immemorial?"

"O, no, indeed. Do get up. You can't think how funny you look. No one kneels now, except in church. If any one were to catch you in that position, I should die of shame."

"Very well, Mrs. Aldwyn; very well, madam," exclaimed Mr. Bunster, wrathfully, as he scrambled to his feet. "You may live to regret that you treated my proposal with so much scorn."

"O, no; not scorn, Mr. Bunster; believe me. But you forget how short a time has elapsed since the Professor departed this life. Only three months! What would the world say if it saw me accepting sweets from you, or any other marrying man, so very soon?"

"Three months," repeated Bunster. "Three days, ma'am, would be too long, in my opinion, to mourn for such a man—"

"*What!*" cried the Professor, springing forward as if he would have seized Bunster by the throat. "And this was my own particular friend—the man who used to dine at my house five days out of the seven, and who borrowed all my instruments from me, as well as half my ideas. Let me only get at him, and I'll shake the life out of him."

"Just so," said John Forest; "but that 'only' is an effectual barrier, I am afraid. You may grasp him as much as you like, Henry Aldwyn. He will only feel a current of air at his throat, and look round to see where the draught comes in. You will do yourself more good by listening to what he says."

"—a man," went on Bunster, "who denied you every reasonable enjoyment; who boasted to his male acquaintances how he had curbed and broken your spirit, as he did that of the dumb brutes in his vivisecting trough, until you knew no will but his own; who was so mean, that he would not spend as much on your pleasure in a year as he did on his own experiments in a day; who—"

"Mr. Bunster," interposed Ethel, proudly, "whatever my late husband's faults may have been, it is not my part to discuss them with you, nor yours to remind me of them. You have exceeded the mission on which you came here, sir. Be good enough to leave me now to myself."

Approaching the bell, she rang it, and simply saying the word "door" to the servant, she bowed to her retreating guest, who had no alternative but to take the hint so decidedly offered him and quit her presence.

Ethel half laughed and half cried when she found herself alone. The interview had made her quite hysterical, and she could not help wondering if Mr. Robson were coming on the same errand. But two in one day. It would be ridiculous. It could never be.

Mr. Robson was as punctual as Mr. Bunster had been. They were both business men, and could not afford to waste their time. Robson was a very different looking person from Bunster. He was gaunt and tall, with a lantern-jaw, and red hair. His age might have been about forty. In years, he would have been a more suitable match for the Professor's widow; but he had no money, and marriage had never entered his head.

"I asked to see you early, Mrs. Aldwyn," he commenced,

"because my business with you is of a delicate nature, and will not brook interruption."

At this address, Ethel made sure he was going to imitate the example of his predecessor, and had almost forestalled his proposal by telling him it was of no use his making it. How glad she was afterwards that she had not done so.

"Indeed, Mr. Robson," she replied; "and what may that be?"

"I trust I shall not hurt your feelings, my dear lady; but of that, I fancy, there is little fear. I wanted to ask you if (the Professor having now been gone for three months) there is not a chance of his library coming to the hammer?"

"O, the books," said Ethel, much relieved. "I'm sure I cannot tell you, Mr. Robson. In fact, I have not thought of it."

"But surely you are not going to keep all those scientific works, which can have no value whatever in a lady's eyes?"

"No, I suppose not. But I am not sure to whom they will eventually belong. The late Professor's children inherit the property at my death. Perhaps we have no right to sell anything out of the house."

Robson looked disappointed.

"There are some books amongst them," he said, "that would be worth any money to a student of science."

"You mean my late husband's writings, I suppose?" said Ethel, timidly.

The Professor saw Robson smile sardonically.

"The Professor's? O, yes!" he replied, shrugging his shoulders. "They are all very well, I daresay, for a student—a beginner—in the abstruse sciences, and I believe he thought very highly of them himself. Most men do of their own works; but, my dear madam, it has not been left for me to tell you surely that your late husband was but a dabbler in his profession."

"*A Dabbler!*" shrieked the voiceless Professor. "*I*; who wrote 'On Subcutaneous Nervi' and 'The Aorta of Tadpoles and Other Germs'! O, this man is insulting my memory. How dare he defame the dead in this atrocious manner?"

"They dare a great many things when they believe they are un-heard," remarked his guide.

"This is by no means the worst you will have to hear of yourself. It's of no use getting in a rage over it. No one will be the wiser for your doing so, and you will lose, perhaps, the gist of the conversation."

"I don't profess to know anything about such things," replied Ethel. "But I thought people considered him clever. It is not *his* works, then, that you desire to possess?"

"*His* works! no. I wouldn't light my fire with them. But he has some valuable books in his collection; and, if they are to be sold, I should like to purchase them by private contract, or have early information of when they will be put up to auction. Will you oblige me by making a note of this, Mrs. Aldwyn, and acting accordingly?"

"I will, with pleasure, Mr. Robson. I feel sure that, if his library is ever dispersed, my late husband would far rather the books went into the hands of an old friend, like yourself, than those of a stranger."

"No! no! no! I wouldn't! He shan't have them! Traitor! Defamer! Liar!" yelled the Professor, as he foamed at the mouth with impotent rage. But his execrations were borne away on the air, and died on the balmy breeze which floated in at the open window.

"I would give a handsome sum for the orthodox ones, Mrs. Aldwyn; but none of *his*—none of the rubbish, remember," said Robson.

"I won't forget," replied Ethel, smiling, just as if he had paid the greatest possible compliment to the ability of her late husband.

"And, now that we have discussed that little matter," said Mr. Robson, "may I ask how you and the young lady are getting on?"

"Very well, indeed," answered Ethel. "We are the best of friends, and never quarrel."

"Ah, poor things, you had enough of that, I guess, in the old days. Pity the Professor made himself so universally disliked, for he wasn't a fool by any manner of means, but terribly inflated with the idea of his own wisdom. However, if he had unbent a little more, there were many men—men of real genius, and no pretense about it—who would have taken him by the hand and given him a lift; but, there, you see, he imagined he knew everything; and this sort of men never grow any wiser to their life's end. I expect he has had his eyes considerably opened by this time. You're none the worse off for his having gone, *I* know," said Robson, winking at the widow.

"I don't pretend to be inconsolable, Mr. Robson," said Ethel, in reply; "but I would rather think as kindly of my husband as I can, now he is no more. We all have our faults, you know, but *his* certainly did not consist of a want of hospitality towards yourself. I think he thoroughly believed in you as his friend, and, I am sure, he did all he could to please you. *You*, therefore, are not the person to try and decry him in the eyes of his widow."

"No more I am," exclaimed Robson, suddenly; "and, by Jove, madam, you have made me feel ashamed of myself. Will you pardon me? Professor Aldwyn, although no scientist, except in his own ideas, was a hospitable friend to me and others like me, and I ought to have bitten out my tongue before I mentioned him in such a manner before you to-day. I really don't know how to make any excuse for myself. The words slipped out before I was aware."

"You have said quite enough, Mr. Robson, and I accept your apology," replied Ethel; "and now, as we have made up our little difference, will you stay and have some luncheon with Miss Aldwyn and myself? She is out just now, but I fully expect her back to lunch. You will be surprised, I am sure, to see the alteration these few months have made in her. She seems to have developed into such a woman since her father's death. All trace of childhood has gone."

"You mean that she has unfolded like a blossom beneath the sunshine of your maternal care?" said Mr. Robson, gallantly.

"That is very prettily put," replied Ethel, smiling, "but I really believe it is true. We love each other, and both the children sadly needed affection."

"Have you had any tidings of the son yet?"

"No; but we hope to have very soon. My solicitors seem quite confident that he went to sea, and that, as soon as he hears of the Professor's death, he will return home."

"Yes, yes, no doubt. It will be a very different home now from what it was before."

At this moment Madeline entered the room, looking flushed and excited.

"Ah, Maddy, you are just in time for luncheon. Mr. Robson will stay and take it with us. You remember your father's friend, Mr. Robson, don't you?"

"Why, certainly. Did he not dine here the very night papa died? How are you, Mr. Robson? I am very glad to see you," she said, holding out her hand, and then she stooped and whispered to Ethel: "All right, eh? Is this the favoured one?" and nearly sent her step-mother off into a fit of laughing in the face of her guest. However, luncheon was happily announced about the same time, and, in the discussion of fricasseed chicken and game, Mr. Robson, who was a regular glutton, forgot to inquire the reason of their mirth.

As soon as they had got rid of him, Maddy burst out:

"O, Mumsey, why did you ask that old horror to stay to lunch? I was bursting to tell you my news all the time."

"Well, dear, I thought I could hardly do less. He arrived just at lunch-time, you see, and having been such an intimate friend of papa's "Well, he's gone at last, thank goodness, though I really thought he had no intention of moving whilst there was a bone left on the table. So, now, let us shut the door and be quite by ourselves."

"I've seen Mrs. Blewitt, of course, and the lady who says she is my mother, and she told me that dear Gillie is on a ship in the Malacca Straits,[33] acting as cook boy (Can you imagine anything more horrible?), and the ship is loading with opium, and the smell has made him quite sick, and he won't be home again for many months, because the ship is going from China to the United States."

"O, Maddy, I am sorry to hear that. I wonder if it is true. I had so hoped the dear boy would have returned to us this summer."

"Of course, I can only tell you what my mother said to me,"

---

[33] The Malacca Straits is the shortest sea route between India, China and Indonesia. The straits are one of the most important shipping lanes in the world for the movement of traded goods.

replied the girl; "but she seemed to know all about him. She told me he had grown very thin and weak since leaving home; that the work had been far too hard for him, and the society he has to keep is something too dreadful to mention. Fancy our poor Gillie, who was so delicately inclined that he turned sick at the sight of blood, and could not bear to hear swearing, or bad language, being subjected to such horrors. I often told him that I was more like a boy than he was, and used to indulge in a big, big D— sometimes, just for the fun of shocking him."

"I know you did, you naughty girl! And your account would make me more unhappy than it does, if I did not think that evil of any sort would run off Gilbert's mind like water from a duck's back. It will make him very unhappy, though, and I shall be more anxious than ever to see him safely home again. If we *only* could communicate with him. Did you ask Susan to tell you the name of his ship?"

"I did, indeed. It was one of the first questions I put to her; but either she could not tell me, or she would not."

"But, my dear, that is very strange. If she can see Gillie and the ship where he is, how is it she cannot tell its name? I can't understand that."

"No more can I," responded Madeline.

The Professor looked towards his guide for an explanation.

"Why is it?" he asked. " It seems as incomprehensible to me as to them."

"That is because you know no more than they do—indeed, a great deal less than they do—of the spiritual laws. The reason is, because spirits can only divulge what they are allowed to do. If they told everything, the designs of the Almighty might be frustrated."

"How?"

"I will take the case of your son, as an example. What would be the consequence if Susan had told Madeline the name of his ship? Ethel would at once have written to him (or wired, more likely) the news of your death, entreating him to return to England at once."

"And why should he not do so?"

"Because it is intended that he shall suffer, as well as yourself, for the incident that took him away from home. If you were cruel and insulting, Gilbert was rebellious against due authority. We are directed to open his eyes a little more plainly to the folly of his behaviour, before he returns to all the luxuries of home. For this purpose, he will have to make the voyage to America, as designed, before reaching England. By that time he will have suffered so much inconvenience and hardship that he will be ready almost to return, like the prodigal son in the Bible, saying: 'Father, I have sinned against heaven and before thee.'[34] Mind, I do not say that were you still on earth he *would* do so, only that he will have been so humbled by the experiences he will have passed through as to be ready to do it."

"May I know how many months more he will be absent from home?"

"Certainly; for you are destined to pass them with him. Gilbert will not step on English ground till you have been in your grave for a year."

"And I am destined, you say, to pass these months by his side?"

"You are. It is ordained that you shall visit him, and I do not think you will wish to leave him again until his surroundings are less dangerous. At present, the poor lad is ill and threatened with fever."

"Let us go to him at once."

"By all means," replied his guide. "Every good wish that you express you will always find gratified. Just place your hand on mine."

The Professor did as he was desired—he experienced a sensation as though he were floating dreamily through a bath of warm, scented air—and, when he opened his eyes again, he found he was standing, with John Forest, on the deck of a second-class trading vessel.

---

[34] The parable of the Prodigal Son is told in Luke, chpt 15, v. 11-32.

- CHAPTER ELEVEN -

IN THE STRAITS OF MALACCA

W hen Gilbert Aldwyn ran out of his father's house he was so excited he hardly knew what he was doing. He was only sixteen, and a very delicate and sensitive lad for his age. He had never shifted for himself in any way before; and he had no idea what he should do or where he should go. But the insult which had been offered to the memory of his dead mother was more than the boy's proud spirit could stand. He had but the faintest recollection of her—the recollection of a child of six years old—but the loyalty with which most young men regard the name of their mother; the pride which will not brook a slur upon her fair fame; the contempt with which they must regard the craven who attempts to insult and annoy them at her expense, were all burning in his youthful breast, as he turned his back, with scorn, on the Professor's dwelling place. He was sorry to leave Madeline and his step-mother—more sorry afterwards than he had time at the moment to realize—but he would have parted with a thousand friends (however dearly he loved them) rather than have stayed to hear his dead mother defamed by the man whose crust he ate and whose roof sheltered him.

As he left what had been his home, he ran for some distance, almost rejoicing at the ease with which he quitted it, and the distance he could put between his father and himself. But, after awhile, he stopped running and began to consider what he should do, where he should go, and how find work wherewith to support himself. At this thought Gilbert halted and sat down on a bench to recover his breath. He found he was in the Embankment Gardens.[35] He had run for a couple of miles without stopping, and

---

[35] Embankment Gardens is a public park by the Thames created in the late nineteenth century.

felt disposed for a rest. He put his hand in his pocket and drew thence three shillings and ninepence. That was the extent of his stock in trade. How much he regretted that he had not carried his savings box, which contained four pounds ten shillings, with him. He had been on the point of taking the money out of it the day before in order to purchase a fishing rod and line, but something had prevented him. It was just like his luck, thought Gilbert, and now "Old Cheese-parings," as he irreverently called the Professor, would have the benefit of his savings. Well, it couldn't be helped, and, if he could only make enough money to keep his soul in his body, he should not regret its loss.

His wish was, of course, to go to sea. What lad, leaving his home in an unorthodox manner, does not regard the sea as his haven of success? Gilbert knew nothing of a seafaring life. He had not even a friend, or a relation of whom he could have taken counsel on the subject. All his knowledge had been gathered from books, where runaway lads became captains of their own vessels in a few years, and rise rapidly to fame and prosperity.

But he knew so far, that the vessels that are about to leave London lie at anchor in the docks at Millwall, or down the river at Tilbury. So he determined to go to Millwall first.

A few inquiries from a friendly policeman, who was taken in by his gentlemanly appearance to believe his story, that he simply wanted to visit a young friend whose ship was lying there, soon gained him the necessary information how to get to the docks by the Metropolitan railway,[36] and in another hour he was walking disconsolately up and down the wilderness of planking and the forest of masts, that seem to constitute the docks of London. He was dressed so well that no one would have thought he was in search of employment, until he timidly ventured to enter one of the offices and ask if they could tell him of any ship on which it was likely he should get work. But the clerk in attendance put so many questions to him, and scrutinized his appearance so narrowly, that Gilbert grew frightened lest he should discover his identity

---

[36] The Metropolitan Railway opened the world's first underground, passenger carrying line in 1863 in central London.

and send him back to his father; and a sudden thought of this kind made him give a false name when asked what he called himself.

The appellation of the young hero in the last boy's book he had read on the subject flashed into his mind, and he answered, "John Dare," before he knew what he was about.

"Ah, well, Mr. John Dare," replied the shipping clerk, "if you want to go to sea, my advice to you is, to go back to your friends and get them to 'prentice you properly, and not let you hang about the docks as if you had left home without leave."

This remark, which hit the truth so nearly, sent poor Gilbert flying out of the office again, in case the intelligent clerk might consider it his duty to make his story patent to the police.

He wandered about till nightfall without meeting with any success, and then felt compelled to creep into one of the drinking houses just outside the docks, which are frequented by the lowest class of sailors and their associates. It was a rough, disreputable place, but the woman who kept it had a kind heart, and the lad's dejected appearance and neat clothing struck her at once.

She made him as comfortable as she could, drawing him away from the crowd of coarse men and women in the front parlour into her private room at the back, and her sympathy was so great that, in a very short time, she had heard, with the exception of his right name, all Gilbert's sad little story.

"Why, my dear," she exclaimed, when he had finished, "you'll never get no work whilst you show yourself in them togs. Any one could see you was a gentleman's kid at once, and would do their level best to keep you out. If you wants low work you must dress accordin'."

"But what am I to do?" said Gillie, looking ruefully at his nice tweed suit and white collar and cuffs "I have no shabby clothes. I wish I had."

"Well, if that's the trouble, I daresay I can help you. I've a son about your size, and I'd be main glad to get your suit for him for Sundays. So if you feel inclined to swop I would give you two sets of Joe's duds for them. You'd want a change aboard; 'twouldn't never do to start with only one. When I says sets I mean a couple of bags, and two jackets and two jumpers. You could keep your shirt, though it's a deal too good for sea, and socks and shoes for when you go ashore. What do you say to the bargain?"

"I'll be very glad to let you have them if they will prevent my getting work, and the sooner we make the exchange the better."

The woman quickly got down the dirty suits which she called "Joe's duds," and swapped them for Gillie's clothes, which had cost three pound ten a short time before.

"And now I'll tell you what," remarked the woman, who was infinitely pleased with her bargain, as she had every reason to be: "my brother, he's boatswain[37] aboard the 'Anne of Hungary,' which is due to sail to-morrer; and he's the man, if any, to let us know if there's any likely work for you about here. Mark, he's in the bar now, and as soon as I can get speech of him I'll let you know what he says. And while I'm gone you'd better slip into them things and tie the rest up into a bundle, ready to take with you, in case you have to start sudden-like."

She bustled away, and Gilbert commenced the distasteful task of arraying himself in "Joe's duds," which were not only ragged and worn, but coated with dirt. The smell of them alone made him sick, and more than once he felt as if it were impossible to wear them, and he must get back into his own clothes. But the thought of work, which he must procure unless he intended to starve, returned to his mind and prevented so rash an act. He was seated in infinite discomfort when his landlady returned, accompanied by her brother.

"Now, here's the devil's own luck for you, mister," she began. "My brother, here, tells me he come ashore a purpus to look for a cook's boy, as theirn has run away at the last minnit. Here is the young man, Mark," she went on, intimating Gilbert with her hand. "And he looks a likely 'un to me, for all he wants a bit o' fattenin', and feeding up."

"Well, he'll have plenty of opportunities for to fatten hisself in the cook's galley," replied Mark, who was a bluff, good-natured looking fellow, not unlike his sister. "And wheere have you bin pickin' up your livin', young un', may I ask? Are you new to the

---

[37] The boatswain was the ship's officer in charge of equipment and crew.

sea?"

"O, quite, sir," replied Gilbert; "but I should like to go to sea very much indeed."

"O, that's wot you think, is it? Well, theere's nothin like tryin'. You've never seen a cook's galley, I fancy?"

"No, never. Shall I have to help to cook? I know how to cook some things, but not many."

"You'll have to obey orders, my lad, and do as you're told, or you'll get a taste of the cat. That's wot you'll have to do. Your wages won't be a fortin, but then you'll live like a fightin' cock all the year round, and have a snug bunk to turn into when your work's done. And when we touches shore, that's the time for larks. Lor! it is a jolly life and no mistake. Wot do you say? Will you come along of us?"

"O, yes, yes," replied Gilbert, who had no more notion of what he was about to undertake than the babe who had just entered the world, and was only glad to think he had procured work so soon.

"Well, then my job ashore is finished, and you can just pick up your bundle and come along o' me. By the way, how are you called?"

"John Dare, sir."

"All right, John. Give 'im a drink, Bet, and then we'll be off. Though it's as mild as mother's milk tonight, he seems shiverin' like with cold. Here, my lad, drink off that tot and you'll feel more like a man."

Saying which, Mark Staveley marched off to the "Anne of Hungary" with his new friend trembling in his wake—not trembling with cold or fear, but that strange feeling which some-times comes over us when we have finally decided on taking a step of which we cannot see the end.

The end was a very direful one for him. Delicately nurtured and brought up (for though the Professor was cruel and harsh to his children he had never denied them the necessaries of life), he was as unfitted for such a position as a lad could possibly be. Never accustomed to associate with companions beneath his own station in life, he was now compelled to herd with the lowest and coarsest of mankind. Sailors from every part of the globe—Dutch, German,

Swedish, Chinese—men who were hardly worthy of the name; whose habits were filthy, and conversation obscene, and full of the most blasphemous oaths, which made him shudder to listen to; men whose natures, whatever they were at first, had become lower than those of the beasts that perish; these were the sort of creatures who assembled night after night in the cook's galley and made the air pestilential with their disgusting conversation.

They were not content either that Gilbert (or John, as they called him) should listen to what they said without complaint— they insisted on his taking part in the discourse or being tabooed as a milksop, and an outsider. His speech and manners soon betrayed his origin and bringing up, and made the rough sailors see that he was not one of themselves; but this fact, instead of mollifying, enraged them, and made them determined not to rest till they had pulled down all his nonsense and utterly demoralized him.

They ridiculed the refinement of his manner, and insisted upon his using oaths, as they did. They revenged themselves for every shocked look the poor lad gave, however involuntarily, by tormenting him till he had neither courage to eat or drink. The work was very hard and, of course, Gilbert was utterly unaccustomed to it; but when he was allowed to snatch four or five hours of troubled sleep they would pull him out of his bunk by the heels and put him under the tap, or threaten to throw him overboard unless he repeated sundry blasphemous and filthy words after them. His life was wholly miserable and almost un-endurable, but he knew that if he appealed to higher authority it would be rendered a still greater hell to him, or probably ended altogether.

Because he had innocently said "thank you," for some aid given him when first coming aboard, he had gained the name amongst his comrades of "Mr. Politeful," and every reminiscence of his old life was hailed by the crew with shouts of derision.

His duties consisted, apparently, of waiting on everybody else, and taking the blame for everything that went wrong in the galley and forecastle of the "Anne of Hungary." One of the younger officers of the vessel had noticed him once, and, struck by his intonation, had put a few questions to him relative to his antecedents, but Gilbert had been so reticent, and answered with such evident reluctance, that he had stopped his catechism, respecting the boy's desire for silence.

But one day the brutalities practiced on him reached their climax. The "Anne of Hungary" was lying off the island of Penang,[38] when a seaman named Masters, a powerful, drunken brute, outstayed his leave ashore and climbed up the ship's chains in the middle of the night, cutting down the companion ladder with such rapidity that the officer on watch had no time to recognize him.

He was pretty well assured of his identity, however, and the following morning Masters was had up and informed that his leave was stopped for the future. The man swore he had done nothing to merit the punishment, and, when accused of dereliction of duty the night before, took his solemn oath that he had been in on time, and that the lad, John Dare, was the only hand who had out-stayed his leave. When Gilbert was confronted with his accuser, however, he steadfastly denied the charge, bringing a witness to his presence aboard, and another to prove that when the bells to turn in sounded Nick Masters' bunk was empty. The effect of this was that Gilbert was acquitted and Masters was condemned, upon which he returned to the forecastle, swearing vengeance against his betrayer.

Gilbert did not know what he had brought upon himself, nor how like savage brutes the men aboard a merchant vessel are; but the following night a piercing shriek sounded throughout the "Anne of Hungary," and John Dare, the cook's boy, rushed on deck, screaming with pain. The officer of the watch and several seamen were on the spot at once, and tried to hold the youth in their arms, but it took all their united strength to do so. He tore wildly round and round the deck, attempting to throw himself into the sea, as though the agony he was suffering had maddened him.

---

[38] The Island of Penang – located in Malaysia. Part of the Straits settlement under the British administration in India in 1826. Came under direct British Colonial rule in 1867, not gaining independence until 1957.

At last, however, by main force, they managed to arrest his course, when it was found that some inhuman wretch had taken the opportunity, whilst he was sleeping, to squirt the juice of green chilies into his eyes, thereby causing him the most acute agony, and threatening to destroy his sight altogether. The unfortunate lad was put to bed, and attended to by the ship's doctor; but the author of the outrage, although shrewdly suspected to be Nick Masters, was never discovered, and, therefore, went unpunished. Meanwhile, the pain Gilbert endured, combined with the heat of the climate, threw him into a nervous fever, at intervals of which he was raving, when the Professor was led by John Forest to his side.

At first, the Professor hardly knew where he was, or why he had been brought into such a filthy place as the forecastle of a second-rate merchant vessel. He had never been aboard such a ship during his earthly life, and the smells and sounds confused him.

"Where on earth have you brought me?" was the first question he addressed to his guide, as they stood together on the quarter deck.

"I have brought you to visit your son, Gilbert. I thought you expressed a wish to see him."

"Gilbert! Why, certainly; but what can he be doing here? This is not the officers' quarters of the vessel, surely?"

"It is not. Gilbert did not embark as an officer. He took the first chance of work which presented itself to him—the only chance of living which your treatment had left to him. 'Beggars cannot be choosers,' you know."

At this moment a long wail came on the air, floating towards them from a small, low, ill-flavoured cabin on their right.

"What is that?" demanded the Professor. "It sounded like an animal in pain."

"Ah, *you* should be able to judge of that, shouldn't you? You've heard it more than once. But, this time, you are mistaken. That cry of anguish comes from a higher sort of animal—from, in fact, your son Gilbert."

"Gilbert in that confined, evil-smelling crib?" exclaimed the

Professor, with amazement. "But why? What has he done? Is he imprisoned for any crime?"

"Only for the crime of having you for his father, which hardly can be called such, perhaps. He is not in prison. That is his regular sleeping-place. But he is in great pain, and some danger. Suppose we enter and have a look at him."

Accordingly, the two spirits entered the wretched cabin together, and looked down on Gilbert lying on his uncomfortable pallet. His bed consisted of a thin, hard mattress laid on a bunk of deal boards; his pillow was a bolster stuffed with wool; he wore no night shirt, but only a coarse, woollen vest, open at the chest, and his whole appearance was dirty and squalid.

But the most pitiable change of all was in his personal appearance. He was thin and emaciated to a degree. The hard fare had not agreed with him. He could not stomach nor digest it, and the hard work had done the rest. Gilbert was, evidently, on the high road to a consumption. His sightless eyes were closed and swollen; his aching head was constantly moving from side to side in a vain quest for repose, and his white face and skeleton arms were sufficient appeal in themselves against the cruelty of those who had driven a delicately-nurtured lad to such a condition.

- CHAPTER TWELVE -

ONE EARNEST WISH TO RISE

"My God!" exclaimed the Professor, as he gazed with horror on the prostrate form of his only son. "Who has done this?"

"*You*," replied John Forest.

"O, no; that is not just. I reprimanded him, it is true; but I never thought it would drive him to such a course. And then I was cut off so suddenly, remember. I had no time given me to remedy the mistake which I had made. Had I been spared for a few days longer, I should, in all probability, have sought him out and rescued him from such a terrible fate."

"You would not; but that is not the point at issue. None of us know, Henry Aldwyn, when we commit an error, if we shall be spared to rectify it. You could not foresee the evils your harshness would produce. So far, you are correct; but you know that your harshness itself was wrong, therefore you are accountable for what followed it. I repeat (and I speak by virtue of the orders given me from above) that you are the only person to blame for Gilbert lying here at the point of death."

"Can I do him no good?" asked the Professor, as he drew closer to the bunk wherein his son lay.

"It is too late; but, for your own sake, you may try. Approach him nearer, and mark what effect your proximity has upon him."

The Professor glided to the bunk head, and stood beside Gilbert. In a moment, his fever broke into delirium.

"Take him away!" he shrieked, at the pitch of his voice. "He is going to destroy my sight again! Ah! have pity! mercy! What have I done that you should torture me like this? Mercy! mercy! O if I could only die and end it all!"

"Your presence does not seem to have a soothing effect upon the patient, does it?" said John Forest.

"No; I will move further off. Poor lad! poor lad! But tell me what brought him to such a terrible state?"

"Principally, as I have already said, your own conduct. But the secondary agent was the brutality of a vicious comrade, who had a grudge against him—a comrade, mind, whom Gilbert would never have associated with, unless it had been for you."

"Yes, yes; I understand," replied the Professor in a low, quivering tone.

At this moment an old sailor entered the cabin, and sat down by Gilbert's side.

"Well, my lad," he said, tenderly, "and hows't be this arternoon? Fairly?"

"O, no, Bennett; I am in agony. I believe my eyes are both burnt out. I cannot sleep for the pain they give me. Shall I ever be well again, do you think?"

"Well again, my boy? Aye; well and bonny as ever. But must have a little patience. I know 'tis hard to bear—summat awful—aye. But 'twill all be over soon, and by the time we touches England's shores agen thou'lt have thy eyesight to greet thy mother with; never fear."

"I have no mother," replied Gilbert, mournfully.

"Thy feyther, then."

"I have no father," repeated the lad, "or worse than none. If it had not been for my father I should never have found myself in this plight. Don't mention him to me, pray."

"Aye, lad, but I thought it wor summat of that sort as druv thee to sea. I guessed from the fust minnit I clapped eyes on 'un ye wern't of ourn sort. Too much the gennelman, lad; that's why they've all spited thee so sorely. But never heed 'un. Un's done theer wust. Take a drink of this lemonade. I coaxed the lemons out of the cook for thee. It'll freshen thee oop a bit."

"How good you are to me, Bennett. What should I have done without your kind nursing? It seems absurd of me to say so now, but if ever I *can* repay you I will."

"Most assuredly he should be repaid," said the Professor to his guide. "Would it not be possible to influence Ethel or Madeline to do so? Is that not some of the work spirits are sent back to earth for?"

"Occasionally, but not spirits such as you. You have never done a good work yourself yet. How then can you hope or expect to be able to influence others to do them? But do not be afraid that Bennett will lose his reward. Every cup of cold water given to a suffering fellow-creature in love and charity is noted down by the recording angel. He is a good, old man, full of kindness and benevolence for all who suffer and who are weaker than himself. He will shine hereafter as one of the stars in heaven."

"*Repay* me, lad?" said Bennett, in answer to Gilbert's last words. "My best payment would be to see thee with a little more hope and courage. Thou'st been cruelly treated, and theer's not a man aboard, as is fit to be called a man, as does not feel for thee. The capen said something yesterday aboot leaving thee ashore in the hospital in Calcutta, and I don't know as it wouldn't be the best thing for thee. Wot dost think thyself?"

"I don't want to leave you, Bennett. I shall feel so lost, blind and alone, in a hospital in a strange country, so far from all I care for."

"Wouldst rather go back to thy feyther, then?" asked the sailor.

"*Go back to my father!* O what are you talking of? I would rather die a thousand deaths than do that. He hates me, Bennett. He told me so. He broke my poor mother's heart, and then he dared to defame her memory before me, her son. I struck him for it, and there's an end of all things between us. I wish, sometimes, I had killed him instead of only striking him. It would have served him right."

"No, no, lad; thou mustn't say that. Feyther's a feyther when all's said and done. I daresay 'un deserved it, but ye mustn't think o' thot. Think of the sweet mother up above. That'll bring better thoughts than the old devil of a feyther, I know."

"Bennett, do you think that angels ever return from heaven to comfort those they have left behind? For I could almost fancy, sometimes, that my mother has been about me whilst I have been lying here, blind and helpless. I have felt soft touches on my brow, and such a soothing sense of peace and quietude. Could it be possible that she has revisited me in this sore distress?"

121

"Possible, my lad," replied the seaman. "Aye, I wouldn't say it isn't; for my own mother came to see me onst when I was in sore trouble, having just berried my poor wife, arter she had been in her own grave a power of five and twenty years. So I shouldn't think it at all unlikely as thy mother haven't come, as mine did, to try and comfort her poor lad."

At that moment the Professor saw the form of Susan Clumber at the head of Gilbert's bed, smiling at her son as she laid her spirit hand upon his aching brow.

"I seem as if I felt her now," murmured the boy, dreamily, "so soft and gentle and loving. Ah, mother, mother, if you had only lived, all this misery would never have been. I would have gone away with you, darling mother, and we would have lived and worked for each other."

"Poor lad! poor lad!" repeated the Professor. "Tell me, John Forest, how soon can we get him out of this terrible plight, and send him home?"

"Gilbert has a penance to perform, as well as you, and will have to work it out to the bitter end," replied his guide. "He will lie on this sick-bed for several weeks more—sometimes raving in delirium, and sometimes too prostrate with fever to be able either to speak or think. The vessel will proceed on her settled voyage, returning to England in about five months' time, when Gilbert will hear of your death and rejoin his sister and step-mother."

"Five months!" repeated the Professor. "Five months of this torture and hardship! But his constitution will never stand it. He will break down under the strain."

"He will, considerably. More than you imagine. His eyesight is nearly destroyed. It will be years before his eyes are really useful to him again; and, in effect, they will never entirely recover from the shock to which they have been subjected. His constitution, also, will suffer from the hardships he has endured aboard this vessel, and he will not be a strong man to his life's end. All this he will owe to you, his father, and will remember it against you till you meet again. Not a pleasant prospect for a young fellow just starting in life, is it?"

"But is there no remedy?" exclaimed the Professor. "Can no

self-sacrifice on my part undo the evils of which I have been guilty?"

"What idea have you in your head? What do you propose to do?"

The Professor thought for a moment, and then replied:

"If I could, by any possibility, show myself to him—spirits have done so before, evidently, by what the old sailor said—might not the sight of me, by convincing him of my death, make him easier with regard to his future?"

"You can try the experiment, if you like," said John Forest; "but I am not very hopeful of the consequences. Stop a minute. You cannot appear as you are now. You would frighten the lad into a premature grave. You must clothe yourself."

"But *how?* I cannot assume mortal habiliments."

"You can think of them, and you will appear to be clothed with them. What was the most usual dress in which your son saw you whilst on earth?"

"Why, usually, I think, in a dressing-gown and slippers."

"The style of dress a self-indulgent man generally assumes. Well, think of your latest dressing-gown and slippers, and I will enable him to see you in them. Stand there, at the foot of his bed, and I will stand by you. When you are ready, I will cause you to appear."

"But how do you do it?" inquired the Professor curiously.

"It is very easy: only like turning on an electric light, and turning it off again."

"Why cannot I do it for myself, then?"

"Because *something* cannot come out of *nothing*, my friend. You have no light to spare from your spiritual body. It is pretty well all dark there—only enough glimmer to carry on your existence with—and none to spare for others. Have you got your dressing-gown and slippers on?"

"I have thought of them," replied the Professor.

In another minute, Gilbert was heard to exclaim:

"Good heavens! There is my father. I am sure of it. I could not mistake him—he made me too miserable. Take him away, Bennett, for God's sake. Don't let him stand there, sneering at me. O! I am mad. I am delirious. But I see him as plainly as ever I did in my life."

"Your feyther, young 'un, d'ye say? Maybe it's his wraith come to warn ye of his death. Gie a good look at un. Doe 'e look live-like?"

"Alive? Yes, far too much alive. Just as he used to look in the horrible days that I shudder to think of. Go and stand there, Bennett, at the foot of the bunk, and shut him out. I cannot bear the sight. It will drive me mad."

"Maybe the poor gentleman has come to tell 'ee he's gone to another world, and to ask 'ee to forgive his bad doin's," suggested Bennett. But Gilbert would not hear of it.

"No, no such luck. Nothing of the sort. He isn't one of the kind either to die or to be sorry for what he has done. He's as hard as the nether millstone,[39] I tell you. He has no heart, no soul. He never had. If he comes again I'll kill myself and end it."

"I don't think your apparition has done your son much good, do you?" said John Forest. But the unhappy Professor had sunk on his knees and was holding up his hands to heaven.

"O, my God!" he cried. "Don't let my son suffer any more for my sins. If it be possible, let my spirit inhabit his body till he reaches his home again, and suffer all that may be before him yet. Accept me instead of Gilbert. Let me expiate the sins of which I am the instigator."

"That is very nice of you to suggest," remarked his guide; "but you will find in this world that the Almighty Spirit does not accept the sacrifice of one man for the sins of another. That would be neither just nor satisfactory. What would Gilbert be the better for your working out the penance he has incurred? Would his spirit be purified because yours suffered pain and hardship? You don't understand these things yet. But the idea was a good one. It was a step in the right direction. I do not despair but that you will short-en your own punishment yet."

The Professor had become very thoughtful. In his mind's eye he could recall the day when his only son was born, and how

---

[39] See Job chpt 41, v. 24 'His heart is as firm as a stone; yea, as hard as a piece of the nether millstone.'

proud he felt—much as he disliked babies and all tender, weak creatures—that he had begotten an heir, to live after him, and perhaps inherit his powers of mind as well as his worldly wealth. He had pictured to himself the little red-faced atom of humanity becoming a learned professor or a great botanist or physician, or a scientist of some sort—that he would educate himself and teach all that he had acquired. And then the years had rolled on and the education had commenced, and he, the father, had tired of the trouble and patience it entailed, and his uncontrollable temper had come in the way, and the child had been frightened and alienated and handed over to the care of strangers.

And this was the end of it. This was his botanist, his philosopher, his electrician; lying, half blinded for life, on a miserable, filthy bunk of a trading vessel, surrounded by beasts rather than men, and dependent for all love and friendship and nursing on an old, unlettered seaman.

In one moment his spiritual eyes seemed to open—the scales fell from them, and he saw himself and his past life as they were—abhorrent in the eyes of God, as he had made them in the sight of men. He perceived, as in a nightmare dream, how much too late it was to remedy the evil he had done on earth, how it would permeate throughout the coming ages, even unto the third and fourth generation. He saw Madeline led, by her mother's teachings, to understand how undesirable a marriage with young Reynolds would be; led by his past teachings to fear and distrust all men and all unions, except such as would bring her worldly gain, until she gave up the idea of marriage altogether, and resolved to live only for her brother's sake. He saw Gilbert, that brother, reaching home after many trials of health and strength, moral as well as physical, half blind and wholly an invalid, unfitted to take his place in the world as a man of talent should—enervated by the hardships he had passed through, and too feeble in body and indolent in mind to care to try and surmount the difficulties in his path. This was what his scientist—his philosopher—his man of fame and genius had come to—and all through his fault—the fault he had no power to undo.

He was not permitted to see further into the future than this; to have been shown his children, overcoming the woeful heritage he had bequeathed to them, and happily mated to true companions and friends, would have been to let him see too much, to have made him too well content to trust to the giver of all good to let things right themselves at last. But the time was not yet come for the Professor to thank God for this.

"I see it all," he cried to John Forest, "you need point out no more to me. I see *myself*, and you could show me nothing more hateful to me. How could I have been so blind, so deaf, so soulless as not to perceive the knowledge that might have saved me? No wonder that Susan will not communicate with me; that I made Ethel wretched; that my own father turns from me with abhorrence; that my children despise my memory, and dread the idea of meeting me again. I am vile—loathsome—accursed of God and men. My mind has been so inflated with the idea of my genius that I have sacrificed everything to the bauble fame—love and friendship and religion. My acquaintances, who pandered to my vanity and conceit, openly ridicule my absurd pretensions, now that my back is turned. One makes love to my widow, and tells her *her* presence was his only attraction to my house—the other wants to buy my precious library, on which I selfishly spent so much money, whilst I refused my wife and children the innocent pleasures their young lives required, and insolently says that he would not light his fire with the writings which took me so many weary hours of thought and labour to compile. And what will be the end of it? My wife Ethel will marry her first love as soon as she decently can, and my children—my own flesh and blood—will do their utmost to drive all remembrance of me from their hearts. It is my doom, but I deserve it. O God, I acknowledge the justice of Thy decree: 'As ye have sown, so shall ye also reap.'"

"That is very true," replied John Forest; "but, fortunately for you, the day for sowing is not yet past, and there may be a second harvest to make up for the failure of the first."

"I am not worthy to think of, or hope for such a reward," said the penitent Professor; "only let me be purged, as though by fire, from the body of this sin; let me be made less unworthy to serve the God who has done so much for me, and whose goodness I

have so shamefully requited. I lift mine eyes to where He dwells—
I long—I aspire to commence my work of purification, that when
it is finished (however long it may endure) I may be fit to take my
place amongst the lowest of those who serve him. John Forest, my
friend and guide! Tell me what I must do to obtain so great
salvation?"

"You have found it out for yourself, Henry Aldwyn. The words
you have just uttered—the first ardent, unselfish prayer that has
ever come from your lips, is the beginning of your upward
progress. From this moment, I am empowered by the grace of
God to say to you: 'Arise! cast off the chains of sin, and begin your
heavenward course.' It will not be an easy one, but it will be full of
hope. Through each trouble you may have to bear you will keep in
mind the glorious truth, that every mortal into whose nostrils has
been breathed the breath of life must live forever, and, living
forever, must assuredly reach the throne of God at last. Your
mission is to remain on this earth, perhaps for many, many years,
but your work will be sweetened by the knowledge that each day
will bring you nearer home. Go forth then as a fisher of men. Use
your undoubted talent in influencing them for good—in protecting
them from evil—in whispering a warning into their ears when they
are in danger of going wrong—a word of advice when they halt
between two opinions—a sense of peace when they have won a
victory over themselves. Your mission must lie especially amongst
your own kith and kin; for it is they whom you have most wronged,
by your example and precept. It will be great pain to you
sometimes, as it has already been, but you must be encouraged to
bear it patiently from the knowledge that without a cross there will
be no crown—without your purgatory, no reward."

"And do you leave me, John Forest?"

"Such are my orders, since you have no further need of my
guidance, and must accomplish the rest by yourself."

"I am not, then, to have any companionship during the remain-
der of my earthly pilgrimage?"

"Are you willing to tread it thus, alone?"

"I am willing to do anything which the good God desires me to
do. Am I not his slave henceforward?"

"That is well spoken and will not pass unheard. Since you are willing to do His will, God is also willing to do yours. Susan, your first wife, is commissioned to remain by your side whilst the Almighty keeps you on this earth. She may not speak to you, but you will see her and feel her presence wherever you go—her influence will lead you aright—and when you have attained her altitude she will be conscious it has been so, and will welcome you as a friend and fellow-worker. For the present, you will both remain near your son. He will feel your nearness to him, without being able to account for it; and, gradually, he will come to think more kindly of you and the past, which now he shudders at. Farewell! My task is ended for the present. Doubtless, I shall meet you again before we are reunited in the spirit world, but, for the moment, other duties call me away. May the blessing of God Almighty rest upon you, Henry Aldwyn, now and for all eternity."

The Professor fell humbly on his knees, hiding his face in his hands, and when he looked up again he was alone. John Forest had returned to the spirit world, but on him there rested a bright ray of sunshine, a reflection of the smile which God had smiled upon His repentant child.

THE END

Appendix A

Science versus Spiritualism – the debate

The dealings of science with Spiritualism form an instructive chapter in the history of human thought. Not the least instructive feature of the chronicle is the sharp contrast between the tone and temper of those men of science who, after examination, accepted, and of those who, with or without examination, rejected the evidence for the alleged physical phenomena. Those who held themselves justified in believing in a new physical force – for de Morgan, Crookes, and other scientific converts did not at the outset, nor in some cases at all, adopt the Spiritualist belief proper – showed in their writings a modesty, candour, and freedom from pre-possession, which shine the more conspicuously by comparison with the blustering arrogance of some of the self-constituted champions of scientific orthodoxy.

from Frank Podmore, *Modern Spiritualism: A History and a Criticism* vol ii (London: Methuen & Co, 1902), p.141.

In 1869, however, an inquiry on an extended scale was undertaken. In January of that year the London Dialectical Society appointed a committee to investigate the alleged phenomena. The committee, as ultimately constituted, consisted of some thirty odd persons, of whom the most notable were A. R. Wallace, Serjeant Cox, Charles Bradlaugh, H. G. Atkinson, Dr James Edmunds, and several other physicians and surgeons. The committee invited the co-operation of Professor Huxley and G. H. Lewes, but both declined, the former on the ground that 'supposing the phenomena to be genuine, they do not interest me. If anybody would endow me with the faculty of listening to the chatter of old women and curates in the nearest cathedral town, I should decline the privilege, having better things to do.'

The committee's labours extended over eighteen months. Evidence, oral or written, was received from a large number of persons who believed the phenomenon to be genuine, but the committee explained that they had 'almost wholly failed to obtain evidence from those who attributed them to fraud or delusion.' The committee further investigated the matter experimentally by means of six sub-committees, who were at liberty to invite mediums and other persons to assist in their researches.

In the event the committee reported that the great majority of their number had themselves witnessed several phases of the phenomena without the presence of any professional medium, and that the evidence thus obtained appeared to establish, amongst other things, the occurrence of sounds and movements of heavy bodies without the use of mechanical contrivance, or the exertion of adequate muscular force. In conclusion, the committee, taking into consideration the high character and great intelligence of many of the witnesses to the more extraordinary facts, the extent to which their testimony is supported by the reports of the sub-committees, and the absence of any proof of imposture or delusion as regards a large portion of the phenomena; and further, having regard to the exceptional character of the phenomena, the large number of persons in every grade of society and over the whole civilised world who are more or less influenced by a belief in their supernatural origin, and to the fact that no philosophical explanation of them has yet been arrived at, deem it incumbent upon them to state their conviction that the subject is worthy of more serious and careful investigation than it has hitherto received.

from Frank Podmore, *Modern Spiritualism: A History and a Criticism* vol ii (London: Methuen & Co, 1902), p. 148.

We commend to our readers in search of the marvellous two papers written by Mr. ALFRED WALLACE in the May and June numbers of the *Fortnightly Review* "On Modern Spiritualism." In these the most astounding statements are made with such calm assurance and confidence that we are really at a loss to say whether the general experience of the human race is to be cast aside as worthless, or whether we are to admit the possibility of events taking place which are in point of fact miracles, and which are stated to be vouched for by large numbers of men who, apparently possessing sound faculties, have commenced as sceptics, have used every effort to discover deception, and have ended by becoming believers. We have used the term "miracle" advisedly, for many of the facts described in these remarkable papers can only be classed as miracles. A table rises up; an accordion performs; a bell rings without being touched by human hands; a red-hot coal is placed on an old gentleman's head, yet fails to injure the skin or singe the hair; flowers consisting of anemones, tulips, chrysanthemums, Chinese primroses, and several ferns, absolutely fresh as if just gathered from a conservatory, appear where none were present before, and under circumstances that Mr. WALLACE believes excluded all possible trickery. A friend asks for a sunflower, and one six feet high falls upon the table, having a large mass of earth about the roots. In such statements as these we have the strangest association of the material and immaterial world – a relation which, to the ordinary scientific mind, is absolutely and entirely inconceivable. But more remains to be told. The phenomena hitherto alluded to were effected chiefly, if not exclusively, by invisible and intangible agents. But with the discovering of new subjects, endowed with the extraordinary powers of a medium, fresh phenomena have been observed. Luminous appearances of various kinds have been seen, followed by the apparition of hands, of faces, and finally of human forms – in one instance sufficiently solid to be embraced by Mr. CROOKES, - usually covered with flowing drapery. Fragments of these spiritual garments have in some instances been cut off by enterprising seers, but have unfortunately always melted away before their texture could be satisfactorily determined. ...

From 'Modern Spiritualism', *Lancet*, June 13, 1874, p. 843.

The quasi-scientific phase of 'spiritualism' alone concerns us here; and the incongruous appeals of 'spiritualists' that 'spiritualism' should be subjected to scientific examination. What can science have to do with people who start with an impudent verbal subterfuge, by converting to their own use a well-known philosophical term – 'spiritualism,' – and seeking thus to give a veneer of probability to their imaginations? In the same way, Mr. Serjeant Cox includes his so-called *psychic force* and *psychism* under the general term *psychology,* and proposes to found a *psychological society* for the study of this *psychic force*, thus playing upon the well-understood word *psychology* to give a certain seeming countenance to his fancies respecting *psychic force!*

The exquisite absurdity of 'spiritualists' craving for a scientific examination of 'spiritualism' and mediumistic phenomena can only be rightly appreciated by those who know something of the history of 'spiritualists' and their doings. Science could not reasonably hope to do more in the discovery of the nature of 'spiritualistic phenomena' than the high priests of 'spiritualism' themselves. What need, for example, to go beyond the 'spirituality' inspired dicta of the celebrated Poughkeepsie seer, ANDREW JACKSON DAVIS, of whom, Mr. HOWITT writes:-

> His clairvoyance was advanced into clairscience. He beheld all the essential nature of things; saw the interior of man and animals as perfectly as their exterior, and described them in language so correct that the most able technologies could not surpass him. He pointed out the proper remedies for all complaints, and the shops [! "We are a smart people here"] where they were obtained ….. The most distant regions and their various productions were present before him.

The highest efforts of ordinary scientific investigation, it will be admitted must yield place to Mr. DAVIS, and he tells us that of the phenomena of mediumship, 6 per cent. are due to voluntary deception, 54 per cent. to certain material influences which he sums up under the different heads, 'neurological,' 'vital electricity,' 'nerve-psychology' (anticipating Mr. Serjeant Cox), 'cerebro-sympathy,' and 'clairvoyance,' and but 40 per cent. to departed spirits. And in respect to the latter manifestations, after the foregoing wondrous display of terminology, we are not surprised to learn that *'it is not safe'* for mediums to rely upon supposed or possible spiritual impressions *'without the entire approbation of their own judgments and powers of understanding upon what may be thus communicated.'* And as the sum of the whole matter we learn that –

'*It is an unwarrantable thing to look for perfect wisdom, or for instruction much superior to the mental development of the medium.*' Here, then, we have it answered in effect by the greatest of modern seers, a seer stamped as genuine, that the knowledge of the medium is the limit of the supposed spiritual knowledge vouchsafed through him. This removes all difficulties out of the way of a right comprehension of 'spiritualism' and 'spiritualists.' We learn how it is that whatever has outraged common sense on earth, whether in religion, in science, or morals, receives a species of apotheosis at the hands of the 'spiritualists.' Mr. HOWITT discovered much of genuine gospel in Mormonism. Homeopathy, Mesmerism, odylism, and the whole range of pseudo-sciences have received a celestial endorsement. We also can now understand how it is that the 'spirits' are liars, contradictory, often debased, and how it comes to pass that heaven is an imperfect copy of earth. We now can learn how it is that even CHRIST is represented as saying, through one of the most accepted of the 'mediums': 'Man lives in the spheres with all his tastes and fancies. If he could not gratify them it would be no happiness to him to be there.'

From 'Spiritualism' and 'Spiritualists', *Lancet*, Jan. 11, 1873, pp. 60-61.

One word at the outset as to what 'a scientific inquiry' really is. It is not a visitation of *séances*. Facts, or what are stated to be 'facts', may be collected by this *dilettante* process, but, the dictum of Mr. WALLACE notwithstanding, facts, real or alleged, will not satisfy the demand Science just now makes upon the propounders of spiritualism. Moreover, to speak plainly, we do not think persons accustomed to scientific observation, and practised in the art of analytical inquiry as applied to the province of nature, wherein much is inscrutable but nothing untrue, are likely to be good or trustworthy inquirers. The *LANCET* was, years ago, the medium of a remarkably sagacious exposure of spiritualistic imposture in the case of the Sisters O'Key, to which we recently alluded. Professor LANKESTER has just made a similar revelation in *The Times*. Such *exposés* are, however, happily rare, and the qualities required for their accomplishment are not commonly found among men devoted to science. Moreover, little has been, or is likely to be, gained by direct observation. When a man not exceptionally well provided with common sense and acumen takes part in a *séance,* he incurs the risk of placing himself in a strait. He must either refuse credence without being able to assign a valid reason for his unbelief, or he will need to confess himself 'shaken,' when such an avowal involves a surrender of the only scientific position consistent with truth and progress – namely, that nothing can be accepted until it is proved, and nothing given up until it is shown to be false. Again, it is always open to the apostles of spiritualism to allege that a particular practitioner of the modern black art is an enemy in disguise, that he has betrayed the true faith, or that, outside, and unaffected by the malpractices of the charlatans exposed, there lies an element of truth to which science must finally do homage, and wise men will do well to take heed.

...

The 'operation of mind upon matter,' 'the reaction of the psychological and the physical,' are glib phrases on the lips of spiritualists; but what do they mean? Is it an ascertained fact that mind is something independent of matter? That the psyche is no essential part, but only tenant and master, of the body physical? Surely these are not scientific truths, and it is a purely scientific inquiry we are asked to undertake. Before any reasonable man can be justified in employing the supposed action of mind upon matter – discarding the scientific probability that it is in fact *a reaction,* - as an hypothesis to explain the phenomena of spiritualism, he must show that mind is something outside the body, capable of existing in a separate state, and endowed with the wholly exceptional power of moving material objects without material forces. ... We see a man or woman – generally a woman – move and act; she is put to sleep or into a reverie or trance – call it what you please. The process by which this artificial somnolency is produced is perfectly intelligible. Presently she begins to move, to speak, to perform actions, as an ordinary sleep-walker. We are now requested, and, strangely enough, expected to believe, that it is not the person before us acting, but another spirit for the moment occupying and employing her body – with such of the faculties as happen to be sufficiently awake – as an agent. We will not say the assumption is preposterous, but is it not purely arbitrary and gratuitous? Does it not violate every canon of scientific reasoning by passing over the obvious sufficient cause and substituting one which is unnecessary, if not purely imaginary – a procedure opposed to the genius of all science, insulting to common sense, and tributary to no intelligible process of truth-seeking, but a fruitful source and factor of every kind, and the grossest forms, of superstition.

...

Those who dally with 'spiritualism,' without either accepting or rejecting it, are the least respectable and the most mischievous of its supporters. They are always searching, but unable to find, the truth. The reason is obvious. Letting go the principles of natural science, they affect to think it possible there may be something outside and beyond nature which has the power of operating within the sphere of the physical world, but is not itself amenable to natural laws. So many paradoxes heaped together as go to make up the remarkable state of unbelieving credulity to which these minds are reduced, can scarcely be found in juxtaposition elsewhere in the domain of science, real or falsely so called. We hold that this play with a serious question is not only indefensible, but disastrous. It either argues ignorance or strange carelessness. Those who demand a 'scientific inquiry' as to the truth of spiritualism might as well ask for a commission to examine and report upon the verity of any particular form of religious faith, with this difference, that in examining a creed avowedly supernatural, the inquirer is not required – on the contrary, he is forbidden – to carry his reason beyond the threshold of the inquiry, whereas in this case, while the phenomena to be investigated are alleged to be wrought by spiritual influences, the complaint is made that it has not been submitted to scientific tests. It is time the hangers-on of 'spiritualism,' the people who are not prepared to give in their adhesion to the theory, as to a system beyond the reach of sense and reason, were exhibited in their true light. The notion of a scientific association entertaining the proposal to discuss this subject is childish. There are no grounds of discussion. Science has no method or process by which it can deal with the question. At the outset we are brought face to face with facts which render the inquiry impossible. It is not that we discredit the stories told us, but, even if true, they would place the matter beyond scientific scrutiny and control. This is the conclusion to which we are driven at the beginning; and thus ends the attempt to satisfy a demand irrational in itself and impracticable in its requirements. Science can reason from the known to the unknown, but when at the threshold of the new province, it is necessary to abandon all the laws, principles, and traditions of the scientific method; it is not a question whether we are willing or indisposed to proceed – a step forward is impossible.

From 'Spiritualism and Science' *Lancet* Sept. 23, 1876, pp.431-433.

Appendix B

Spirit Photography

We now approach a subject which cannot be omitted in any impartial sketch of the evidences of Spiritualism, since it is that which furnishes perhaps the most unassailable demonstration it is possible to obtain of the objective reality of spiritual forms, and also of the truthful nature of the evidence furnished by seers when they describe figures visible to themselves alone. It has been already indicated – and it is a fact of which the records of Spiritualism furnish ample proof – that different individuals possess the power of seeing such forms and figures in very variable degrees. Thus it often happens at a séance, that some will see distinct lights of which they will describe the form, appearance, position, while others will see nothing at all. If only one or two persons see the lights, the rest will naturally impute it to their imagination; but there are cases in which only one or two of those present are unable to see them. There are also cases in which all see them, but in very different degrees of distinctness; yet that they see the same objects is proved by their all agreeing as to the position and the movement of the lights. Again, what some see as merely luminous clouds, others will see as distinct human forms, either partial or entire. In other cases all present see the form – whether hand, face or entire figure – with equal distinctness. Again, the objective reality of these appearances is sometimes proved by their being touched, or by their being seen to move objects – in some cases heard to speak, in others seen to write, by several persons at one and the same time; the figure seen or the writing produced being sometimes unmistakably recognisable as that of some deceased friend. A volume could easily be filled with records of this class of appearances, authenticated by place, date, and names of witnesses, and a considerable selection is to be found in the works of Mr. Robert Dale Owen.

Now, at this point, an inquirer, who had not prejudged the question, and who did not believe his own knowledge of the universe to be so complete as to justify him in rejecting all evidence for facts which he had hitherto considered to be in the highest degree improbable, might fairly say, 'Your evidence for the appearance of visible, tangible, spiritual forms is very strong; but I should like to have them submitted to a crucial test, which would quite settle the question of the possibility of their being due to a coincident delusion of several senses of several persons at the same time; and, if satisfactory, would demonstrate their objective reality in a way nothing else can do. If they really reflect or emit light which makes them visible to human eyes *they can be photographed.* Photograph them and you will have an unanswerable proof that your human witnesses are trustworthy.' Two years ago we could only have replied to this very proper suggestion, that we believed it had been done and could be again done, but that we had not satisfactory evidence to offer. Now, however, we are in a position to state, not only that it has been frequently done, but that evidence is of such a nature as to satisfy anyone who will take the trouble carefully to examine it. This evidence we will now lay before our readers, and we venture to think they will acknowledge it to be most remarkable.

Before doing so, it may be as well to clear away a popular misconception. Mr G. H. Lewes advised the Dialectical Committee to distinguish carefully between 'facts and inferences from facts.' This is especially necessary in the case of what are called spirit-photographs. The figures which occur in these, when not produced by any human agency, may be of 'spiritual' origin without being figures of 'spirits.' There is much evidence to show that they are, in some cases, forms produced by invisible intelligences, but distinct from them. In other cases the intelligence appears to clothe itself with matter capable of being perceived by us; but even then it does not follow that the form produced is the actual image of the spiritual form. It may be but a reproduction of the former mortal form with its terrestrial accompaniments, *for purposes of recognition.*

Most persons have heard of these 'ghost-pictures,' and how easily they can be made to order by any photographer, and are therefore disposed to think they can be of no use as evidence. But a little consideration will show that the means by which sham ghosts can be manufactured being so well known to all photographers, it becomes easy to apply tests or arrange conditions so as to prevent imposition. The following are some of the more obvious:-

> 1. If a person with a knowledge of photography takes his own glass plates, examines the camera used and all the accessories, and watches the whole process of taking a picture, then, if any definite form appears on the negative beside the sitter, it is a proof that some object was present capable of reflecting or emitting the actinic rays, although invisible to those present. 2. If an unmistakable likeness appears of a deceased person totally unknown to the photographer. 3. If figures appear on the negative having a definite relation to the figure of the sitter, who chooses his own position, attitude, and accompaniments, it is a proof that invisible figures were really there.

Everyone of these tests have now been successfully applied in our own country...

Through an independent set of most competent observers we have the crucial test of photography; a witness which cannot be deceived, which has no preconceived opinions, which cannot register 'subjective' impressions; a thoroughly scientific witness, who is admitted into our law courts, and whose testimony is good as against any number of recollections of what did happen or opinions as to what ought to and must have happened. And what have the other side brought against this overwhelming array of consistent and unimpeachable evidence? They have merely made absurd and inadequate suppositions, but have not disproved or explained away one weighty fact!

My position, therefore, is that the phenomenon of Spiritualism in their entirety do *not* require further confirmation. They are proved quite as well as any facts are proved in other sciences; and it is not denial or quibbling that can disprove any of them, but only fresh facts and accurate deductions from those facts. When the opponents of Spiritualism can give a record of their researches approaching induration and completeness to those of its advocates, and when they can discover and show in detail either how the phenomena are produced or how the many sane and able men here referred to have been deluded into a coincident belief that they have witnessed them, and when they can prove the correctness of their theory by producing a like belief in a body of equally sane and able unbelievers then, and not til then, will it be necessary for spiritualists to produce fresh confirmation of facts which are, and always have been, sufficiently real and indisputable to satisfy any honest and persevering inquiry.

From, Alfred Russel Wallace, *Miracles and Modern Spiritualism* (London: George Redway, 1896), pp. 188 – 193; pp. 211-212..

It is not until 1872, however, that we find any record of spirit photography in this country. The manifestation originated about the same time as the materialisations dealt with in the last chapter, and through the same instrumentality – that of Mr. and Mrs. Guppy. After trial in the domestic circle for some weeks without success, Mr. Guppy found a photographer named Hudson who, with the assistance of Mrs. Guppy or some other medium, was able to produce some spirit pictures. The procedure was much the same as that followed by Mumler. The sitter would be posed in front of the camera, and, if the operation were successful, the developed picture would present, in addition to his own image, another figure, in most cases draped, and with the features blurred or only partly discernible.

Hudson's studio was at once besieged by eager Spiritualists, and numerous testimonies to the genuineness of the results appeared in the Spiritualist papers. Mr Slater, an optician, took his own camera, lenses, and plates, and watched the process throughout, without discovering any suspicious circumstances. Moreover, though most of the spirit faces were more or less veiled in white drapery, a considerable proportion were unhesitatingly recognised by the sitters as the likenesses of friends.

from Frank Podmore, *Modern Spiritualism: A History and a Criticism* vol ii (London: Methuen & Co, 1902), p.118.

In the summer of 1874 a Parisian photographer, one Buguet, had come to London and produced spirit pictures. These pictures were of much higher artistic quality than those proceeding from Hudson's studio; the spirit faces were in most cases clearly defined, and were, in fact, frequently recognised by the sitters, and even W. H. Harrison failed to detect any trickery in the operation. Harrison watched the operation throughout, but was not allowed himself to operate, and for the identification of the glass plate he relied upon a small fragment of glass *broken off by Buguet.* I suspect that, ... Buguet found here an opportunity for substitution.

Many of the recognised figures were, indeed, those of well-known personages. Thus, Allan Kardec appeared on the plate when his widow was the sitter; the same spirit also appeared with Miss Anna Blackwell, his best-known English disciple. Miss Blackwell was also favoured by the presence of Charles Dickens and of King Charles' head. Mr Gledstanes obtained a portrait of the recently deceased Judge Edmonds. Prominent Spiritualists like Lady Caithness, her son, the Duke de Medina Pomar, and the Comte de Bullet, obtained portraits of near relatives. Instances of this kind do not in themselves afford any presumption of supernormal power. Nor, again, is it difficult to account, on they hypothesis of trickery, for the appearance of the well-known features of Stainton Moses himself on the sensitised plate in Buguet's studio in Paris, when the original was, as he tells us, lying in his bed in London in a state of deep trance. It is much more remarkable to find that comparatively obscure persons, of whom it is unlikely that Buguet could have heard, should again and again have obtained recognisable portraits of their dead friends. Out of a hundred and twenty photographs by Buguet dealt with by Stainton Moses, evidence was forthcoming of recognition, or of the operation being produced under test conditions, in as many as forty, a far higher proportion than was the case with Hudson or Parkes.

Stainton Moses' endorsement of Buguet's claims appeared in *Human Nature* for May 1875. In the following month Buguet was arrested and charged by the French Government with the fraudulent manufacture of spirit photographs. When put on his trial Buguet made a full confession. The whole of his 'spirit' photographs were, he stated, produced by means of double exposure. In the first instance he employed his assistants – of whom there were three or four – to play the part of ghost. Later, as his business grew, and he feared that the constant repetition of the same feature might arouse suspicion, he constructed a headless doll or lay figure, which variously draped, served for the body of the ghost. The head was commonly chosen to suit the expectations, where these were expressed, or apparent circumstances of the sitter; information on these points being frequently extracted by the assistants, who receive the visitors on their entrance. The lay figure and a large stock of heads were seized by the police at the studio.

The peculiar interest of the trial did not consist, however, in these paltry revelations; for, after all, Buguet did little to improve on the methods inaugurated by his predecessors. It is the effect produced on his dupes by Buguet's confession, and the display of his trick apparatus, which is really worthy of attention. Witness after witness – journalist, photographic expert, musician, merchant, man of letters, optician, ex-professor of history, colonel of artillery, etc., etc. – came forward to testify on behalf of the accused. Some had watched the process throughout, and were satisfied that trickery had not been practised. Many had obtained on the plate unmistakable portraits of those dear to them, and found it impossible to relinquish their faith. One after another these witnesses were confronted with Buguet, and heard him explain how the trick had been done. One after another they left the witness-box, protesting that they could not doubt the evidence of their own eyes.

...

The effect of the exposure on English Spiritualists appears to have been much the same as the effect on Buguet's actual dupes. Stainton Moses remarked that the prosecution bore traces of clerical origin, that the judge was strongly biased, and that Buguet was obviously a genuine medium, who had no doubt been bribed or terrorised to make a spurious confession and to fabricate a box full of trick apparatus for exhibition at the trial. William Howitt saw in the whole proceedings further evidence of an organised conspiracy on the part of the Jesuits to overthrow Spiritualism. They had in this instance, he pointed out, apparently bribed a genuine medium to confess to imaginary trickery, as a few years before they had sent one of their own emissaries, Allan Kardec, to poison the pure wells of the new truth with the pestilential doctrine of reincarnation.

However, the result of the trial was undoubtedly on the whole to discourage the profession of spirit photography, and we hear little more of it in this country after 1875.

from Frank Podmore, *Modern Spiritualism: A History and a Criticism* vol ii (London: Methuen & Co, 1902), pp. 120 – 123.

I had just finished taking a picture for a gentleman who resides in Canada, when the door-bell rang, and a lady dressed in black, wearing a crape veil, was ushered in. The veil was so thick it was impossible to distinguish a single feature of her face. Without raising her veil she spoke to the gentleman, for whom I had just taken a picture, saying 'Have you had a picture taken, sir?' He replied in the affirmative. 'Do you recognize it?' she asked. He answered, 'Well, I am not much used to looking at a negative, but I think I know who it is.' Then, turning to me, she said: 'What do you charge for these pictures?' I stated the price, and she decided to sit for one. I requested her to be seated; would be ready for her in a moment. I went into my dark room and coated a plate. When I came out I found her seated, with her veil still over her face. I asked if she intended to have her picture taken with the veil? She replied, 'When you are ready, I will remove it.' I said I was ready, whereupon she removed the veil and the picture was taken. I then requested her name for the purpose of recording it in the engagement book. 'Mrs Lindall' was given. Mrs Lindall asked when she could have the pictures; and was told, in about three days. The negative, marked 'Mrs Lindall', was sent with the others to my printers. The pictures were returned only a few moments before Mrs Lincoln called, and laid on my desk, in envelopes, with the names on the outside that were on the negative – Mrs Lindall's among the rest.[1] I was away at the time, and consequently had not seen the pictures, and did not recognise the form on her negative, as I had not the slightest idea that I had had such a distinguished sitter.

My wife was engaged in conversation with a lady-friend, when the door-bell rang, and a lady was shown in. She asked if her pictures were ready? My wife asked, 'What name?' The lady replied, 'Mrs Lindall.' Mrs. M then went to my desk, and looking over the packages of pictures, found one marked Mrs. Lindall, which she handed to her, and then continued the conversation with her friend, who, by-the-way, being of an inquisitive turn of mind, asked Mrs. Lincoln (who was at this time examining her picture closely) if she recognized the likeness? Mrs. Lincoln replied, hesitatingly, 'Yes.' My wife was almost instantly entranced, and, turning to Mrs. Lincoln said 'Mother, if you cannot recognize father, show the picture to Robert; he will recognize it.' 'Yes-yes, dear' Mrs Lincoln said; 'I do recognize it; but who is now speaking?' she asked. The control replied: 'Thaddeus!' A long conversation ensued. Mr Lincoln afterwards controlled and talked with her – so the lady-friend informed me who had thus unexpectedly been a witness of this excellent test.

When my wife resumed her normal condition, she found Mrs Lincoln weeping tears of joy that she had again found her loved ones, and apparently anxious to learn, if possible, how long before she could join them in their spirit home. But this information could of course not be given. Mrs Lincoln then related how she left Springfield, Ill., for the sole purpose of visiting my studio, and having a picture taken as a test. For that express purpose she travelled *in cog*. When she arrived in Boston, she came directly to my house, before visiting a hotel, for fear that some one who knew her might see and recognize her, and thus defeat the object for which she had taken such a long journey.

The picture of Mr. Lincoln is an excellent one. He is seen standing

---

[1] The writer regularly moves between using the lady's assumed name and real name.

behind her, with his hands resting on her shoulders, and looking down, with a pleasant smile.

William H Mumler, *The Personal Experiences of William. H. Mumler in Spirit-Photography. Written by Himself* (Boston: Colby & Rich, 1875), pp. 29-31.

Appendix C

Extracts from Florence Marryat's *There Is No Death*

Apropos of these still-born children, I had a curious experience with Mrs. Fitzgerald. I had had no idea until then that children so born possessed any souls, or lived again, but 'Florence' undeceived me when she told me she had charge of her little brothers and sisters. She even professed to know the names by which they were known in the spirit world. When a still-born baby is launched upon the other side, she said it is delivered over to the nearest relative of its parent, to be called by what name he may choose. Thus my first girl was christened by Colonel Lean's mother 'Gertrude,' after a bosom friend of hers, and my second my father named 'Joan,' as he said it was his favourite female name. Upon subsequent inquiry, we found that Mrs. Lean had a friend called 'Gertrude,' and that 'Joan' was distinctly Captain Marryat's *beau ideal* of a woman's name. However, that signified but little. I became very curious to see or speak with these unknown babies of mine, and used to worry 'Florence' to bring them to me. She would expostulate with me after this fashion: 'Dear mother, be reasonable. Remember what babies they are, and that this world is quite strange to them. When your earthly children were small you never allowed them to be brought down before strangers, for fear they should cry. 'Gertie' and 'Yonnie' would behave just the same if I brought them back to you now.' However, I went on teasing her till she made the attempt, and 'Gertie' returned through Mrs. Fitzgerald. It was a long time before we could coax her to remain with us, and when she overcame her first shyness, it was like talking to a little savage. 'Gertie' didn't know the meaning of anything, or the names of anything. Her incessant questions of 'What's a father?' 'What is a mother?' 'What's a dog?' were very difficult to answer; but she would chatter about the spirit-world, and what she did there, as glibly as possible. She told us that she knew her brother Francis (the lad who was drowned at sea) very well, and she 'ran races, and Francis chivvied her; and when he caught her, he held her under the fountain, and the spray wetted her frock, and made it look like silver.' The word 'chivied' sounded to me very much of a mundane character, I asked 'Gertie' where she learned it; and she said, 'Francis says 'chivy' so I may,' and it was indeed a common expression with him. 'Gertie' took, after a while, such a keen interest in my ornaments and china, rather to their endangerment, that I bought a doll to see if she would play with it. At first she was vastly delighted with the 'little spirit,' as she called it, and nursed it just as a mortal child would have done. But when she began to question me as to the reason the doll did not look at her, or answer her, or move about, and I said it was because it was not alive, she was dreadfully disappointed. 'Not alive!' she echoed; 'didn't God make it?' and when I replied in the negative, she threw it to the other end of the room, and would never look at it again.

'Gertie' was about five years old at this period, and seemed to have a great idea of her own importance. She always announced herself as 'The Princess Gertie,' and was very dignified in her behaviour. One day, when a lady friend was present when 'Gertie' came and asked her to kiss her, she extended her hand instead of her face, saying, 'You may kiss my hand.'

'Yonnie' (as 'Joan' called herself) was but eighteen months old, and used to manifest herself, *roaring* like a child forcibly dragged before strangers, and the only word we could ever extract from her was 'Sugar-plums.' Accordingly, I invested in some for her benefit, with which she filled her mouth so full as nearly to choke the medium, and 'Florence' rebuked me seriously for my carelessness, and threatened never to bring 'Yonnie' down to this earth again. There had been three other children – boys – whom I was equally anxious to see again, but, for some inexplicable reason, 'Florence' said it was impossible that they could manifest. The little girls, however, came until we were quite familiar with them. I am aware that all this must sound very childish, but had it not borne a remarkable context, I should not have related it.   (pp. 157-159)

* * * * *

Another medium, whose health paid the sacrifice demanded of her for the exhibition of a power over which, at one time, she had no control, and which never brought her in anything but the thanks of her friends, is Mrs. Keningale Cook (Mabel Collins), whom I have mentioned in the 'Story of my Spirit Child.' There was a photographer in London, named Hudson, who had been very successful in developing spirit photographs. He would prepare to take an ordinary photograph, and on developing the plate, one or more spirit forms would be found standing by the sitter, in which forms were recognized the faces of deceased friends. Of course, the generality of people said that the plates were prepared beforehand with vague misty figures, and the imagination of the sitter did the rest. I had been for some time anxious to test Mr. Hudson's powers for myself, and one morning very early, between nine and ten o'clock, I asked Mrs. Cook, as a medium, to accompany me to his studio. He was not personally acquainted with either of us, and we went so early that we found him rather unwilling to set to work. Indeed, at first he declined. We disturbed him at breakfast and in his shirt sleeves, and he told us his studio had been freshly painted, and it was quite impossible to use it until dry. But we pressed him to take our photographs until he consented, and we ascended to the studio. It was certainly very difficult to avoid painting ourselves, and the screen placed behind was perfectly wet. We had not mentioned a word to Mr. Hudson about spirit photographs, and the first plate he took out and held up to the light, we saw him draw his coat sleeve across. When we asked him what he was doing, he turned to us and said, 'Are you ladies Spiritualists?' When we answered in the affirmative, he continued, 'I rubbed out the plate because I thought there was something on it, and most sitters would object. I often have to destroy three or four negatives before I get a clear picture.' We begged him not to rub out any more as we were curious to see the results. He, consequently, developed three of us, sitting side by side. The first was too indistinct to be of any use. It represented us, with a third form, merely a patch of white, lying on the ground, whilst a mass of hair was over my knee. 'Florence' afterwards informed me that this was an attempt to depict herself. The second picture showed Mrs. Cook and myself as before, with 'Charlie' standing behind me. I have spoken of 'Charlie' (Stephen Charles Bernard Abbott) in

'Curious Coincidences,' and how much he was attached to me and mine. In the photograph he is represented in his cowl and monk's frock – with ropes around his waist, and his face looking down. In the third picture, an old lady in a net cap and white shawl was standing with her two hands on Mrs. Cook's shoulders. This was her grandmother, and the profile was so distinctly delineated, that her father, Mr. Mortimer Collins, recognized it at once as the portrait of his mother. The old lady had been a member of the Plymouth Brethren sect, and wore the identical shawl of white silk with an embroidered border which she used to wear during her last years on earth. I have seen many other spirit photographs taken by Mr. Hudson, but I adhere to my resolution to speak only of that which I have proved by the exercise of my own senses. I have the two photographs I mention to this day, and have often wished that Mr. Hudson's removal from town had not prevented my sitting again to him in order to procure the likenesses of other friends. (pp. 185-187).

Victorian Secrets

www.victoriansecrets.co.uk

Victorian Secrets revives neglected nineteenth-century works and makes them available to the modern reader.

New titles are under development all the time. An up-to-date catalogue can be found on the website.

If you would like to suggest a title for publication, please contact us at suggestions@victoriansecrets.co.uk

Should you find any major errors in this book, please let us know at feedback@victoriansecrets.co.uk

Lightning Source UK Ltd.
Milton Keynes UK
UKHW020635230921
391069UK00011B/767